Scandalous

Victoria Christopher Murray

Chapter 1

These strippers didn't have a thing on me.

I had to fight hard not to roll my eyes as the faux-cop on the stage twirled his baton as if he was about to arrest somebody. Then, he smacked that wood in the palm of his hand and sent the one hundred or so women who had packed the strip club on Sunset Boulevard into a frenzy.

"Oh, my," Kyla Blake squealed when the dancer came to the edge of the stage and gyrated right in front of us wearing nothing but his black silk thong and police hat. His hips circled one way while he whipped that baton over his head in the other direction.

Kyla giggled, then closed one eye as if peeking like a cyclops was far less sinful. Beside her, Alexis Ward had both of her eyes wide open as she buckled over with laughter. Looking at the two of them finally made me roll my eyes.

Silly women!

What were they howling at? That naked cop, with his hairless chest and shoulder-length Jheri curl, barely looked like he was sixteen.

I shook my head. I'd always known that Kyla, who'd been my best friend since kindergarten, had lived a highly sheltered life. So for her to be sitting up in this club and giggling like a school girl at this school boy wasn't surprising. But Alexis...I don't know who she thought she was fooling. Everyone saw Alexis, Kyla's other best friend, as this sophisticated Southern belle, teeming with purity. Please! I knew better. I was sure that this wasn't her first time in a strip club. In fact, I wouldn't have been surprised if I ever found out that she'd once taken to the pole exactly the way I had.

I was so far into my head and my thoughts that I didn't realize everyone at the table was pointing at me. I looked up and right in front of my eyes was the center of that black silk thong.

"So, you're the birthday girl?" the naked policeman yelled down to me from the stage in such a high-pitched voice that I wondered if he really *was* sixteen.

I hesitated for a moment, but it was only because I had to hold back my yawn. "It's not my birthday," I said in a tone that was meant to dismiss him. "I'm getting married."

But that didn't make him back up, which led me to believe that one of these foolish girls Kyla invited to my bachelorette party must be paying him a little extra so that he would jump down from the stage and fall right into my lap.

What kind of place was this? Over at Foxtails, where I'd been a...*dancer*...for the last four years, we didn't just come off the stage like this. No, not at all. As strippers, we had class...and we had rules. No fraternizing with the patrons from the stage – except of course when you came to the edge to collect those tips that the men tucked inside your G-string.

But obviously, this place didn't have the kind of class that I was used to working with. The nine women sitting around the table with me cheered as the stripper danced all over me.

"So ya getting married?" he asked with his face so close to mine that I could almost smell his mother's milk still on his breath. How old was this guy? I mean, he'd looked young on the stage, but up close and personal, he looked like he'd just learned to brush his teeth.

I pushed back in the chair, kinda surprised at the way he was coming at me. This was another thing that we didn't do at Foxtails – no touching – except when you were invited into the red-curtained VIP Room, of course.

"Let me give you something to remember me by," the kid said.

Kyla's friends ('cause really, these women sitting here at this table, that's who they were – not one of these women could say that they really liked me) all howled as the stripper leaned back as if he was about to go under a limbo pole and made his pecs jump and his thighs quiver to the beat of the music.

The women applauded and I couldn't help it: I yawned. I didn't even try to hide it. I just opened my mouth and let my lips stretch wide. And I got all into that yawn, too. I moaned and groaned, releasing all of my boredom.

His look of hurt was instant and right away, I felt bad. But it wasn't my fault. I mean, how were you gonna bring a stripper to a strip club and expect her to be entertained? Now granted, Kyla didn't know that I was a stripper. No one knew that. But still, she knew who I was. She knew that I wouldn't be impressed by a bunch of naked men. Please, before she and I had graduated from high school I'd already seen – and had – my share.

But the poor boy had really been trying to impress me and once my yawn came out, it was all over for him. I guess it was different for guys than it was for us girls. When I was stripping, there were many times when I would dance onto that stage and some of the men wouldn't even look at me. They were either talking to their buddies or focusing on the girls who were working the floor. That's when I'd come up with my booty quake. I'd done it my very first time on the stage, but once I saw how those dudes tossed twenties at me when I did that, I became the booty quake specialist. That move became my signature and men from all over Southern California came to see me quiver my butt like I was part of the San Andreas Fault. After a couple of months, whenever I came out, the club went silent except for the music and the cat calls. The talking? I shut it all down. Every man in that club – and the few women who were there – paid attention when I, Pepper Pulaski, strutted onto the stage.

So this young man, if he was gonna last, was gonna have to grow some skin that was thicker than what he had. What he needed to do was suck it up and find a way to come up with something that could catch even my attention. But for right now, this boy couldn't do a thing for me, because I was, after all, Jasmine Cox. And you had to bring it far better than that to impress me.

I didn't want him to walk away feeling too bad, though. So, when he looked at me like he was about to cry, I smiled, and then started praying for his song and dance to come to an end.

"Let's hear it for Robocop."

Throughout the club, the women cheered as if Robo was part of the delegation for the second coming. I still felt bad as the young man gathered the bills that had fallen from his G-string and then trotted off the stage as if he was in a hurry. I wondered if he was rushing off to finish his homework back stage.

But whatever, at least this night was finally over. I was sure that was the last set; I'd sat through twelve dancers, and not a one of them could have stood next to me on the stage, at least not when it came to stripping. I had turned my college occupation into an art form; I had researched, studied, and rehearsed until I became the best in the business. So I couldn't really blame any of these young men who obviously hadn't put in the time that I had.

Anyway, I was ready to rise on up out of here.

Then, a siren blared through the club as red, white, and blue strobe lights circled through the darkness giving me an instant headache. It wasn't the blasting music or the psychedelic colors that made me sick. It was the fact that the night had not yet come to an end.

"Fire!"

"That's my song," Kyla said. She jumped up and started swiveling her narrow hips as she raised her hands high above her head. If I didn't know better, I would've thought my girl was drunk. But that concoction that she loved so much (orange and cranberry juice) couldn't hurt a five-year-old.

I sighed.

"Ladies," the DJ yelled out, "get ready for Fire Cracker!"

Oh, lawd! What was I gonna do? I wasn't about to sit through another amateur set because if I did, I would....

Then, he walked onto the stage.

The screams were so loud the walls vibrated.

"The way you walk and talk really sets me off to a full alarm, child." Kyla, still on her feet, sang along with the Ohio Players record that the DJ was spinning.

But I hardly heard the music anymore. My eyes were on him.

"Him" was a six-three, two-hundred and forty pound hunk of solid, dark Godiva chocolate. Oh yeah, I could assess them like that. Being a stripper had given me the ability to hone in on those kinds of stats in three seconds flat. I'd learned how to appraise men for many reasons, including the part of my work that sometimes came after my dancing and often took place in the VIP lounge. I had to learn how to judge a book by his cover: physically, mentally, financially, especially.

And I loved this chocolate cover!

Mr. Chocolate (which was much more appropriate to me than Fire Cracker) was dressed in full fireman's gear that began to drop, piece by piece, as the Ohio players sang and these women in the club screamed for him to go ahead and get naked. I almost jumped up with them – if the outside looked this good, I couldn't wait to see what he was working with.

"The way you squeeze and tease...."

Mr. Chocolate dropped to his knees and then without holding on to a single thing, rose slowly, slowly, slowly until he was standing and just wearing his fireman's pants.

The women erupted in delight.

And though I didn't applaud, I was pleased, too. And impressed. Just like everyone else, I was on the edge of my seat, mesmerized by Mr. Chocolate's talents.

His talents included looking like he'd been carved out of a solid brick of chocolate. Everything about him looked as if God was using him to show the rest of humanity what a real man should be.

From his bodybuilder's biceps to his shaped and bulging triceps, quads and hamstrings, to his pecs that were perfection, Mr. Chocolate was a flawless man. But the best part for me was his head – completely shaven like he was Mr. Clean, and looking as soft as a baby's bottom.

Dang! All the brothers I knew were still rocking Jheri curls and the newest fad, the high-top fade. But obviously Mr. Chocolate didn't follow the masses. It was 1987 and he was marching to his own drum, and I wouldn't be surprised if by 1988 every man who had come within two feet of Mr. Chocolate had started shaving their heads, too.

Around me, the women were screaming and stomping like animals. Through my peripheral vision, I saw that even Kyla Carrington (I still hadn't gotten used to calling her by her married name) was panting like a dog in heat. And that was huge because I knew for a fact that her husband, the up-and-coming Dr. Jefferson Blake, was the only man that she had ever had sex with. Was she fantasizing about someone else for the first time in her life?

But thoughts of my best friend flew right out of my head when Mr. Chocolate looked straight down at me; I would've dropped my panties right there if he had asked me. It was his eyes. I was completely taken by this man's eyes. I'm telling you, Mr. Chocolate was a delicious piece of the finest dark candy that you would ever find, but his eyes were the color of freshly watered spring grass.

I'd never seen anyone with skin as dark as his with sparkling green eyes.

The Ohio Players sang, "When you push, push...." and Mr. Chocolate dropped his pants.

It was official: I was in love.

He came to the edge of the stage, right above where I was sitting, and he gave me a wonderful view of his complete magnificence. Daannnggg! I knew this man had to be mine –

But then I coughed and reeled back that thought. Yes, I was absolutely used to getting any man I wanted. But no, I couldn't do that anymore.

I was getting married in two days.

In forty-eight hours, I would have a husband I was supposed to love, honor and obey. That meant that I had to give up all of this extra-curricular sextivity. Right?

Right! I repeated to myself. Right! Right! Right!

I kept up that mantra as Mr. Chocolate grinded. I kept up that mantra as Mr. Chocolate bucked. I kept up that mantra until Mr. Chocolate danced right off the stage.

I couldn't even move. Not for a couple of minutes. I had to wait, to get myself together and get my mind right before I was able to stand up.

Just ten minutes before, I'd been thinking that this was the worst bachelorette party ever. But those six blessed minutes that Mr. Chocolate had given me made it worth the whole night.

I grabbed my sweater and just tossed it over my shoulders. It wasn't that I needed it. Not only had it been one of those dog-hot August days, but Mr. Chocolate had warmed me up so much I was about to start taking off some clothes myself.

Around me, the girls were still cackling and giggling, comparing how many dollar bills they had left. I hoped I was going to be able to sneak away without having to go through a bunch of goodbyes and well wishes from these heifers who would be lying through their teeth if they said anything nice to me. Not one of Kyla's friends liked me. Because of their husbands and boyfriends, of course.

Not that I cared what these females thought, but them not liking me wasn't really my fault. I couldn't help the fact that I was a man-magnet wherever I went, even if it was just to a party at Kyla and Jefferson's house. Whenever I was around, their men were always all up in my Kool-Aid. But like I said, not my fault. That drama belonged to them.

I decided that I could walk right out of the club without having to say anything. But just as I turned away from the table, Kyla yelled out, "Jasmine!"

Dang! My hope had been to jet on out of here with just visions of Mr. Chocolate on my mind. I couldn't turn away from my best friend, though, so I did a little pirouette on my tippy-toes and faced Kyla with a smile.

She was still grinning as she stepped to me. I'm telling you, she had never seen anything like this show before.

"I hope you enjoyed your party," she gushed as she hugged me.

"I did, girl."

"You know I wanted to give you something bigger but...."

I held up my hand. "This was enough."

It was true that Kyla had wanted to plan some elaborate affair for me because that was just who she was. But really, who was gonna come? It had already been proven that I didn't have many...okay, I didn't have *any* female friends. Kyla had sent out fifty invitations for my bridal shower and only she and Alexis had shown up. And I would've bet that she'd paid Alexis to be there, which was a waste of money because I wanted to pay Alexis to leave.

So I didn't want Kyla to go through the trouble of a no-show bachelorette party. But Kyla, being Kyla, had to do something, and she had come up with the perfect way to get her friends to attend. Naked men always attract desperate women.

I really loved my friend who would do anything for me. Few understood our friendship: the good girl and her morally-corrupt sidekick. The thing was, though, Kyla and I had a history. It had begun when I had to beat-down some little boy for picking on the new girl in our kindergarten class; she'd been grateful that day, and our friendship had blossomed from there. Even though she was the privileged child of Lynn and Winston Carrington, Kyla treated me so much like a sister that her parents began to treat me like their daughter. But though their intentions were always good, I was always aware that I was a Cox, not a Carrington. There was nothing white about my parents' blue-collar jobs. Our house was barely one thousand square feet and couldn't compare to the expansive three-bedroom home where she'd grown up. The only thing I ever had over Kyla was my social abilities: I had boyfriends. Not that the boys didn't want her – by the time we hit fifth grade, it killed me the way the boys constantly drooled over her.

The thing was, Kyla wasn't giving up anything. I, on the other hand, had no problem with giving it and getting it. Some girls called me a slut, others said I was a ho. But whatever the name, I was the most popular girl in high school. I was so popular that I'd snagged our school's star jock, Kenneth Larson. Not only had I snagged him, but Kenny and I had gone to USC together, where I had to fight hard to keep him. But I did. And he had put that ring on my finger.

The star jock part – where he was supposed to be drafted into the NFL – didn't quite work out after he was injured in his first bowl game. But he was still Kenny Larson, the ex-USC football superstar. And he was still going to be my husband.

"I hope you're not getting ready to leave," Kyla said, tugging me away from my thoughts. "I have one final surprise for you."

I guess my plans to sneak out and just call Kyla later were now derailed. In my mind, I was already preparing the lie for whatever plans she had, the reason why I couldn't go out to dinner with them, or go somewhere for a drink with them, or whatever it was that Kyla wanted to do.

"You know what?" I began my lie, "I've got to get over to my dad's because – "

Kyla spoke over me. "But I've arranged for us to meet the dancers."

I zipped my mouth shut for a moment to make sure that I'd heard her right. "What did you say?"

She grinned and nodded. "Surprise!" she said in her kooky kind of way. "You know, since you wouldn't let me do anything really special for your bachelorette party, I thought this would be just a little extra nice surprise. Just for us to get together for a little while."

"So, the dancers are gonna come out here now?" I asked so that I could get clarification.

She nodded like a bobble-head.

"They let you meet the dancers here?" I asked, really surprised.

"Yeah." She frowned. "You say that like it's strange or something."

"It is. In these kinds of places, the dancers are not supposed to fraternize with the customers. At least, not in a chatting, getting-to-know-you kind of way."

"As if you're an expert on strip clubs." Kyla laughed.

I did not laugh with her.

After she giggled for a few more moments, she waved her hand and said, "Please. I am Doctor Jefferson Blake's wife."

I grinned. "Oh, so Jefferson is an expert on strip clubs."

"No, but the owner is a patient of his. So, I got the hook-up. They arranged this little get-together. It's not gonna be that long or elaborate. But the guys are gonna come out and say hello." Her smile faded and she pouted a little in the way that only Kyla Blake could. "So please stay. Just for a little while. Please?"

I slipped that sweater right off my shoulders. She didn't have to beg me twice. "Okay." I let the word drag out of me. "I'll stay," I said as if it was going to be a chore and not a pleasure.

"Great," Kyla said, right before one of the girls who'd come to my party – I couldn't even remember her name – called Kyla back over to the table.

As she turned back to her friends, I headed toward the bar. So I was gonna get a chance to meet Mr. Chocolate personally? Oh, yeah.

I edged up to the bar, glad that there was no one standing there. I knew how to work this thing. I wanted to be all alone when Mr. Chocolate moseyed into the main part of the club. Even though I always stood out, I wanted him to see me far away from the other *silly* women.

Oh, yeah.

"I'll have a ginger ale," I told the bartender. I'd already had one glass of wine. That was enough. I wanted a clear head, for lots of reasons.

The lights began to brighten in the club. Not too much, but enough for me to take a good glance around.

Clearly, this was more of a club than a strip joint. Where I worked, at Foxtails, it was all about the stage and the girls. Nothing else – except for the bar – mattered.

But here, the emphasis seemed to be on the club itself. There were cloths covering the tables, pictures hanging on the walls, and fresh flowers all around. Flowers in a place where men took off their clothes? I guess here, because they were catering to women, the atmosphere mattered as much as the dancers.

I took a sip of my ginger ale and turned around. Most of the women had left; I guess it was just going to be our group who would have the pleasure of mixing with the strippers.

Kyla and the rest of the girls were still giggling and cackling, even though there was not yet a dancer in sight.

Silly women.

But then, he came out. Mr. Chocolate. He was the first one.

The women clapped as he stepped into their midst, but with just a smile and a nod, he made his way away from where Kyla and her friends stood and came toward the bar. It was as if he was looking for me!

Behind him, the other dancers came out and kept the women's attention away from Mr. Chocolate. So for at least a moment, I was gonna bask in the presence of perfection all by myself.

He didn't even look my way as he leaned against the mahogany bar and said, "Doug, get me a hit."

A hit? What was that? Whatever it was, I wanted to be the one to give it to him.

One of the things that made me so good at being a stripper was that I always played it cool. I kept my feelings to myself – something I'd been doing for the last few years, ever since my mother passed away. After going through her death, there was no one and nothing that could get to me.

But all of my cool was gone right now. Just because I was only inches away from this fine thang. I was staring and raking my brain for the right thing to say, but I couldn't think of anything. Dang! I was acting like all the other women who were here.

Mr. Chocolate had reduced me to a silly woman.

Maybe I needed to turn away for a moment. Maybe I needed to break my eyes away so that I could get myself together. I had never been attracted to any man so instantly. It was like I'd known Mr. Chocolate from before.

I turned away, but only for a couple of seconds before I allowed my eyes to wander, inching down his body bit by bit, until my eyes settled on his shoes. My assessment: he wore a size thirteen, at least.

I sighed as he turned toward me.

"So, you're here with that party?"

Okay Jasmine, I thought to myself. Don't lose any cool points. I took a sip of my soda and let a couple of ice chips settle onto my tongue before I responded.

"Actually, yes," I said, totally composed, totally faking it. "The party is in my honor."

"Ah!" He took a sip of the golden liquid in the screwball glass in front of him. "Well then, happy whatever to you."

"Thank you," I said, glad that he hadn't asked me what kind of party I was being honored with.

He held his hand out to me. "My name is Roman."

I couldn't help it. I laughed.

"So that's funny?" he asked, though he didn't look like he was insulted. His beautiful green eyes sparkled like he wanted in on the joke.

"No...not funny. It's just that I'm not surprised." I paused. "Roman...as in a Roman god?"

He took a longer sip of his drink before he said, "No, Roman as in empire!"

I laughed louder this time. This was my kind of man, 'cause I was all about being on top of everything.

"So," he said. "What's the occasion? What are y'all celebrating?"

It took me a couple of seconds to calculate my answer. I'd already made the mistake of telling him the party was in my honor, but I could easily say I was celebrating a birthday. The problem with that, though, was that there were too many witnesses here, which meant there were too many chances that he'd speak to someone who would tell him different. So, the truth – which didn't always work out so well for me – was what I was left with.

"It's a bachelorette party."

His eyebrows arched upwards as if he couldn't believe it. And then, he did what so many men did: he assessed me, inch by inch, just like I'd done to him a couple of minutes ago. I was glad I'd worn this black Tadashi dress. The spandex told anyone who was looking that I was all woman.

"You're getting married?" he finally asked.

"You say that like you can't believe someone would marry me."

He chuckled. "No, sweetheart, that's not it at all." He took a final swig of his drink before he said, "I know there would be plenty of men who'd want to marry you. I just can't believe that one of them actually caught you." He slid his glass across the bar then stepped closer to me.

My mouth became instantly dry.

There were just a few inches between us when Roman said, "So, Miss...I'm Getting Married. Were you caught? Were you caught, for real?"

In forty-eight hours, I'm getting married. I'm getting married, in forty-eight hours.

My plan was to say that over and over. But the problem was when my eyes focused in on Mr. Chocolate's plump bottom lip, I couldn't get those words to make any kind of sense in my mind.

"So, what do you say?" His voice sounded a little like he had gravel in his mouth. "Are you really gonna get married?"

Then, the tip of his tongue traveled slowly, slowly, slowly across that juicy lip of his.

I was completely done.

Chapter 2

We were at my favorite restaurant – Crustacean's – me and Mr. Chocolate. But we were only there for a few moments before I heard the sound of water, and now the two of us were walking shoulder-to-shoulder, hand-in-hand on the edge of the Pacific. It didn't make a lot of sense, but that was okay with me because I understood where I was: in the nonsensical realm of a dream. And I wasn't about to rush toward consciousness. No, I was too busy enjoying the presence of the man who had been here in my constant state of fantasy for the last ten hours.

Roman had been on and in my mind since I'd left the club last night. At first, my attraction to him had been all about the physical: those green eyes against the palette of his dark skin, and those plump lips that looked like they had been ripened purposely to mate with mine. Usually, that was all that I needed – the fine body of a man. But then Roman and I had talked. And that was when he truly made his way to my...let's just say, my heart.

It was weird the way it happened. The way the two of us stood at that bar together, as if no one else existed. And it was even stranger the way everyone left us alone; the women who'd come to my bachelorette party had forgotten all about me. Their focus was on the other twelve men who had entertained us.

Like I said, that was weird because Roman was the only one who was worth spending any time with, but as was always the case, I had more sense than most females. So I kept Roman to myself and for the minutes that we were together, I fantasized that he was truly all mine. And, then I came home and took that fantasy straight into my dreams. Over and over, I dreamt about our time together at the bar and the perfect way my bachelorette party had ended.

"So, are you going to answer my question?" Roman had said.

"What?" I understood what he was asking me, but I needed to give myself time to come up with the right answer.

He smiled as if he knew that I was stalling and then he stepped even closer to me as if he wanted me to know that he was willing to play my game. "You heard me. Were you caught? Are you trying to tell me that some man truly caught you and now you're his?"

I tried to think about Kenny, I really did. But it was hard to get my mind to focus on my fiancé when all of this fine chocolate was all up in my space! And then, when he leaned back a bit and looked me up and down, like I was a piece...of chocolate, I compromised: I didn't say a thing. Just smiled wide enough to show him that the dimple in my left cheek was as cute as the rest of me, and then sipped the last of my ginger ale.

He laughed as if he got my message and took another swig of his own drink. "We should get to know one another a little bit better. What are you doing this weekend?"

My first thought was to ask why we had to wait for the weekend. It was just nine o'clock; we had the whole night. But I didn't want to look like the hoochie that everyone said I was. Plus, I was about to get married.

So that's what I told Roman. "This weekend...Saturday...I'm getting married."

His eyes widened. "You're getting married *this* weekend?"

"Yeah." I frowned. "What? You didn't believe me?"

"Nah...nah, it's not that. It's just...I didn't expect that it was gonna be so soon." He paused and his eyes took a journey once again all over me. And this time, I wished it was his mouth taking that trip. "So, Saturday, huh? Can I get an invite?"

I chuckled. "I just met you."

"I know, but it doesn't feel that way, does it?"

Was this one of the best come-ons, or was he for real? I wasn't sure at first, but then I remembered where I was, and who Roman was. He was just like me – we were strippers. This conversation was all part of the game: create an amazing fantasy for our customers to get the biggest tip possible.

Even though Mr. Chocolate wasn't about to get any more money out of me, I played along. "You're right. I feel like I've known you for a long time." I lowered my voice, really getting into my part. "Like maybe even from before I was born."

I'd expected him to laugh, chuckle, smile, or something to let me know that he found my words amusing. But he just nodded as if he thought I was serious. Dang, he was really into this role-playing.

And for some reason, that only made me want him more.

Too bad.

But then he said, "Well, your wedding is Saturday...what are you doing tomorrow?"

Okay, until this point, this was just a flirtation. But now it felt as if Roman wanted to make this fantasy real. A one night stand the night before my wedding? I'd be lying if I said that wasn't a tempting thought. Especially since I hadn't had any in three weeks. But the point of my short-term celibacy was to be ready for my husband, so this encounter would have to stay in the flirt a little, fantasize a lot category.

Anything else would be purely scandalous!

"Tomorrow," I said, "I'm going to be getting ready to become a wife."

"Does that take special preparation?"

"For me, it does. I want to be perfect for my husband."

"You look pretty perfect to me."

This time when his eyes wandered over me, I felt as if I'd been caressed – and that was when I knew it was time to stop, before I lost the ability to just say no. I hoisted the strap of my bag onto my shoulder, a clear sign that I was about to make my move and get up out of this joint before trouble swept me away.

"It was really nice to meet you, Roman," I said, holding out my hand to him.

He looked down at my hand and frowned. "Did I say something wrong?"

"No. It's just late and I have to get home," then I paused so that I could make my point, "to my fiancé."

"You live together?"

That question surprised me. Not only was it none of his business, but it went beyond the fantasy. Who cared who lived with whom when you were playing a game?

But maybe male strippers did it differently. So, I answered, "Yeah, and I don't want to keep him up and waiting."

He nodded, but his face drooped a bit, as if he was sad to see me go.

As I tried to saunter past him, he caught my fingers inside his hand and held me there close to him. The heat of his breath warmed my neck when he whispered, "It's too bad we didn't meet sooner. Before now."

Wow! Male strippers took the game all the way to the end. If Roman had still been on the stage and still been naked, I would've been tossing dollars until he had all my money.

Then he added, "You should come and see me sometime...but not here. Down at the beach."

He didn't have to explain anymore. With the way his muscles bulged through his skin and the mention of the beach, I knew what he was talking about. Venice Beach. Muscle Beach – the one that Arnold Schwarzenegger, among others, made famous. I didn't get a chance to get down to the beach too often, but whenever I did that was the first place I stopped. I mean, really. Fine, half-naked men with skin that glistened beneath the baking Southern Cali sun? What self-respecting, men-loving woman wouldn't stop there?

"That's where you work out." It was a statement more than a question.

"Where I work out and where I work. I'm a trainer for the bodybuilders."

I nodded; it figured.

"So, you think you'll come by?"

"Yeah," I said.

He grinned.

I added, "Maybe me and my fiancé will come and check you out." My words were meant to push a stake through the heart of this fantasy – for Roman and for me. It had been fun, but it was over.

"He'll be your husband by then." I guess that was Roman's way of letting me know that the game was over for him, too.

I nodded, smiled, and uncurled my fingers from his grasp. As I made my way over to where Kyla and her silly friends still gathered, I knew Roman's eyes were on me. I could say that I felt them, but I didn't – I just knew. Men were always happy to see me coming, but they were just as thrilled to see me go. It was what I carried in my trunk that had made me all that money as a stripper. That's not conceit; that's just a fact.

"Wow, you were over there talking to him for a long time," Kyla said to me, then giggled.

I wasn't about to explain it to her; I just said, "Turns out we have a few friends in common."

"Really!" Kyla exclaimed. She glanced over to where Roman still stood at the bar. "Who could you two possibly have in common?"

I shook my head. I wasn't offended in any way, though. That was my girl, Kyla. She was bourgie from way back. It was in her genes, from her mother's side of the family, and now that Kyla was a doctor's wife, her head was way up in the sky.

Still, I loved her. How could I not? Kyla was what I called a Big F Friend. Even though her friends didn't like me, that didn't matter to Kyla. She loved me, period. And I had a feeling that if she had to give up all of her friends to stay friends with me, she would do just that.

"Yeah, we do know some of the same people," I said. "He knows a couple of people at my job." Then, because I didn't want to explain or lie any further, I added, "Anyway, let me get out of here. I still have a lot to do before Saturday."

Those words brought out the pout from Kyla that I expected.

"I really wish you would let me stay with you tomorrow. That's what a matron-of-honor is supposed to do. That's what you did when you were my maid-of-honor."

"Yeah, but we're different," I said, stating the obvious. "You wanted company and I want to spend my last night as a single woman by myself to reflect on everything."

"But we can do that together?"

I shook my head then hugged her. "I'm not gonna talk about this anymore. I'm gonna be fine."

"I know you are," Kyla said as she pulled away from our embrace. "Anyway, you wanna wait for a couple of minutes and we'll walk out together? I'm just waiting for Alexis to come out of the bathroom."

I rolled my eyes and that was enough to get my message across.

"Stop it," Kyla said. "I don't know why you and Alexis can't be friends."

"Because I could never befriend anyone who shares the name and characteristics of a female dog."

"Stop it," Kyla said again, but this time, she couldn't hold back her laughter. She may have thought what I'd said was funny, but to me, it was nothing but the truth. I didn't like Alexis. She'd gone to college with Kyla and when she moved to Los Angeles from her native South Carolina, I'd wanted to buy her a one-way ticket back.

I don't know what it was, but from the moment I met Alexis I knew we'd be the best of enemies. Someone looking at me from the outside might say that I was jealous. But you need to know that I wasn't. Just because she was a leggy, model-type brainiac who owned a successful business didn't mean that she had a thing on me. I had it going on, too. Just as many men were sniffin' around me as were sniffin' around her.

Really, to me, the problem was that Alexis was jealous – and scared – of me. She knew that if she ever got a man ('cause as much as she had it going on, she didn't have one), she was afraid that if he got one look at me...well, then.

Just the thought of that made me laugh. "Look," I said to Kyla. "Let me get out of here. I'll see you Saturday."

Kyla hugged me again. "I can't believe you're about to be an old married lady like me."

Like her? Please! No matter how much Kyla wanted us to be alike, we were so far from it.

"Speak for yourself," I said. "I'm never going to be an old anything. I'll call you tomorrow." I turned around and almost bumped right into Roman.

"You're walking out now?" he asked.

"Yeah."

"Well, a lady shouldn't be by herself this late at night. You just never know."

I nodded, because it was easier to let him think I was a lady rather than explain that I'd been on these mean streets plenty of times (later than this) by myself. But I'd let him do the gentlemanly thing just so I could have a few extra minutes with my fantasy.

Together we took two steps before Alexis came barreling around the corner. She glanced at me, then her eyes turned to Roman. And with a shake of her head and a laugh, she pushed past me as if she hadn't been there to celebrate my happy occasion.

I knew what she was thinking: that I was about to do Roman. She thought I was a whore, but she didn't know me at all, 'cause if she did, she'd know that I didn't do that kind of thing for free.

So I just ignored her, and turned my attention back to Mr. Chocolate and our final moments together....

"You awake yet, babe?"

Oh, man. I'd almost forgotten that I was dreaming. I felt like I was right there, right back at last night. But now I was on the verge of consciousness, and I didn't want to wake up. I wasn't finished with reliving the party's last moments.

"Babe?" Kenny called out to me again.

Inside I sighed, really irritated that he was stopping me from getting to my happy ending. I wanted to remember the way Roman had walked silently by my side as we made our way to the parking lot. I wanted to remember the way he'd taken the car key from my hand and unlocked the door, then held it open as I slipped inside. And finally, I wanted to remember the way his fleshy lips felt like satin had brushed across my cheek – my goodnight, goodbye-forever kiss.

Even though that's where last night had ended, my plan had been to continue the dream and take it to that forbidden place: where I would have pulled Roman into the car and he would've had his way with me right there. It wouldn't have been the first time that I'd had sex in a car with a man I'd known for thirty minutes. That was the life of a stripper-plus – which was the name us girls in the industry called ourselves, because we couldn't possibly be compared to the ladies of the night who strolled the streets and congregated on corners. We were on a much higher level.

Anyway, that had been my plan…to dream a little longer and imagine what could have been.

But I didn't get the chance to do any of that, because my betrothed had chosen that moment to come out of the shower and wake me up.

"Babe?"

He was gonna push it 'til I opened my eyes. So I did. I let my lids flutter open slowly, though, as if I'd been in a deep sleep. I milked it too, stretching and moaning as though I was being dragged into consciousness totally against my will.

That was supposed to make Kenny feel bad, so he'd tell me to go back to my sweet dreams. But when my eyes were all the way open, Kenny stood in front of me with a white towel wrapped loosely around his waist and a super-sized grin on his face. I knew what he wanted, but he wasn't gonna get it.

I guess he could see my answer by the look in my eyes.

"Ah, man!" he whined, like he was a kid being denied candy. "You're serious about this, aren't you?"

"What part of 'I want our wedding night to be special' don't you understand?"

He eased down onto the bed and brushed his lips against the same place on my cheek where Roman had left his mark. "Any time you and I are together is special to me," he said, looking into my eyes. "Don't you feel that way too?"

I nodded, even though by agreeing, I was lying. I mean, Kenny really was my hero. He was the best man that I knew. It was just that he didn't do it for me anymore.

Inside, I sighed. I remembered the days when I couldn't get enough of Kenny Larson. From high school until our junior year in college, I could've sexed this man for breakfast, lunch, dinner, and all the snacks in between.

But then came our senior year, and my mother's illness, and incredible medical bills, and her death, and my do-right father who believed that he should never be a debtor. All of that led to the emptying of a college fund that my parents had saved for years, and a hefty tuition bill that had to be paid if I was going to graduate with my class from USC.

And that led to the day I walked into Foxtails, one of the more popular upscale strip clubs in LA, dropped my pants for Buck, the owner, and took off everything else a few hours later for a few hundred men.

But it was in the VIP room where I earned the most. And not just in money. I mean, I was supposed to be back there for the men, but I was getting mine, too. There were men – especially some of the big ballers – who knew how to bring it to a woman. They gave it to me in every way anyone could imagine: lying down, standing up, upside down. There were times when I wanted to give the men their money back, just tell them that the pleasure was all mine. Of course, I never did that, but I made sure that I had seconds, thirds, fourths and beyond with some of those dudes. Those men turned me into a sex-craving woman who'd rather be in a king-sized bed than a five-star restaurant.

I'd had sex with so many men that it got to the point where I had to think about being in that back room when I was in bed with Kenny. Which was why I'd held back my goodies from him for the last three weeks. This was my quest to make our wedding night special, because the truth was that's what I really wanted, and that's what Kenny deserved.

Kenny pressed his lips against mine, but when his tongue started seeking permission to come inside, I pushed myself up and away.

"Not even a kiss?"

"Nope," I said, "because if I start kissing you, I won't want to stop and then it'll be my fault." That was the truth. I was so horny right about now – from my encounter last night, my dream this morning, and the lock I'd put between my legs for the last three weeks – that a kiss would bust me wide open.

"A'right," he said begrudgingly. "But babe, it's gonna be all the way live tomorrow night." He strutted to our walk-in closet as if he was moving to music. His towel was draped so loosely that all I had to do was blow and he'd be butt-naked. But I let him get away because I loved Kenny Larson something fierce and my self-imposed celibacy was part of my plan to get back all the love that I once had for him.

Kenny was the truth when it came to being a good man. He'd taken care of me during my darkest days and it wasn't his fault that I'd ended up finding a whole new life as a dancer at Foxtails. Truly, I wanted to get back to the place where we were before I started cheating on Kenny. Not that I was really cheating-cheating. All the men I'd been with over the last three years were strictly business.

But now that he was claiming me as his wife, I wanted to do right by him. Not sleeping with another man was going to be the easy part. It was getting back those deep-down-to-my-soul feelings for Kenny that were once such a natural part of me.

I was going to do it, though, no matter what. Because I loved him.

My beeper vibrated, and I grabbed it. On the screen was a number I knew all too well. Ugh! Didn't he get it? Didn't he know he wasn't supposed to contact me anymore?

"What's up, babe?" Kenny asked as he stepped out of the closet, fully dressed in one of the suits I'd purchased for him from the Men's Warehouse. That was a step-up from those places where he'd been buying his suits in downtown LA – three for seventy-nine dollars.

"Nothing," I said. "Why?"

"You look like you'd seen a ghost. Who beeped you? Work?"

"Yeah," I said, glad that he'd come up with the lie for me. "I'll call them, but I'm still not going in. Carnation will have to do without me 'cause today is totally about getting myself ready for you."

Those words made him pimp-strut over to the bed. "I like the sound of that," he said. "But you don't have to do anything to get ready. You look pretty perfect to me."

It was a déjà vu moment · one of those times when you knew you'd been in this place before, but just can't remember when. Only I knew exactly when. I was here last night. Kenny had just uttered the same words that Roman had said to me.

I shuddered.

"You cold, babe? The air-conditioning's not on."

"No, no, I'm fine," I said, giving him a very light peck on his lips. "You better get going or you're gonna be late."

He nodded. "I wish I could take today off with you, but I'm using all my time for our honeymoon."

That made me smile. Kenny hadn't told me where we were going yet, and I was enjoying the mystery. It was totally so unlike him. He was always so rock solid, so predictable, so...boring. But keeping the honeymoon a secret spiced things up a bit for me, and it meant a lot that he was trying so hard.

"Are you sure you don't want to tell me where we're going?" I asked for the thousandth time. "How am I suppose to pack?"

He shook his head just like he did all those other times. "This is my surprise and it will not be spoiled, woman," he said, trying to sound like a throwback to caveman days. "I told you. You don't have to pack a thing. I got you!"

That was another thing that made this so great. He was taking care of everything. Usually, I was the one who did the planning, the preparations and, the paying. But with this, Kenny was stepping up.

Even though he wouldn't give me any hints, I clapped my hands like a kid. I was so excited.

Kenny laughed and then hugged me. "This is it," he said.

I stood up so that I could give it to him real. "The next time you'll see me, I'll be your bride."

"You'll be my wife."

With those words, I let him kiss me. How could I not? As we embraced, I remembered all the times we'd had together and remembered why I wanted to marry this man. By the time we pulled away from each other, I was absolutely sure that by this time next week, I'd be all the way back in that loving place.

"Have fun at the hotel tonight," he said.

"I'm not going to be doing anything. I'll just be waiting for tomorrow to come." I kissed him once again and watched him stroll out of our bedroom, so pleased with myself. I was doing the right thing by letting this sexual tension build. Tomorrow it would be on for real.

Then, my beeper vibrated once again. I didn't even have to look down at the number. I knew who was calling.

And it was not good.

Chapter 3

My heart pumped, and my stomach fluttered as I turned my BMW into the parking lot at Foxtails. It had been a while since I'd been here. Once I quit, I didn't look back – that had been my plan, to sever all ties. But then the call had come in this morning from Buck and curiosity replaced the blood in my veins and pumped all through me. I'd called him back the moment Kenny walked out the door.

"Pepper!" he sang when he picked up. "What's happening? You ready to come back to work?"

"Buck, please don't waste my time. I'm only calling 'cause you paged me, twice. What's up with that?"

"Can't an old boss call his best girl?"

"Not for no nonsense," I said, with an attitude.

It still surprised me how I could get away with talking to Buck any ol' way, especially since he scared me to death the first time I'd met him: this big-hipped white boy, with his thick, blond, shoulder-length locks, who talked like a Black man. I'd been shaking when he made me take off my top and drop my pants so that he could check out what I was working with. He'd looked me over like I was a piece of meat, which I guess I was.

Anyway, that was the last time he had me shaking. The only times I shook after that was on stage for money.

I have to admit, though, Buck and I had a special relationship. That man looked out for me. I "dated" a lot of men, but because of Buck, I never felt like I was in any kind of danger. He didn't play that, and those dudes knew it. If anyone ever wanted me to leave the club with them, Buck had to know about it. Had to know who it was, where was I going, and then I had to call and check in once it was over. I always pretended that Buck did that because he cared for me. But I knew what was up. This was all about the Benjamins; Buck had a vested interest. I was, by far, his biggest rainmaker. He couldn't let anything happen to me.

But we had parted ways because I was getting married and I wanted to be the wife who stayed true. So a call from him was not what I wanted the day before my wedding.

"Listen, Buck," I'd said to him. "If you ain't talkin' 'bout nothin', then, I'm gonna hang up."

"No, no, you know I'm just playin'. I do need you to come by the club, though."

"For what?" I put a lot of bass in my voice so that he could hear my frown.

"I got something for you. For your wedding."

I knew that was a lie right off the bat. "Your cheap behind didn't get me a dang-bang thang! If you don't tell me, I'm just gonna hang up and..."

He laughed. "I didn't get you nothin'. You need to be paying me...leaving me and you were my best girl."

I rolled my eyes. How many times was he going to take me back to that? I'd quit Foxtails three months ago, figuring that was going to give me enough time to feel like a virgin again on my wedding night. But that didn't stop Buck from calling and begging me to come back.

Buck just didn't know. It was hard for me to walk away from all of that sex and all of that money. Especially since the star I thought I was marrying never got around to shining. Kenny had taken a job with the *Los Angeles Times* in the finance department. And even though he had a degree from one of the top schools in the country, he had settled for earning only $25,000 a year, half of what I was making at my job at Carnation. It seemed that the man I fell in love with, the man who talked big about living large and having dreams, didn't have very much ambition at all.

I'd thought about calling off our engagement many times – I needed to be married to someone who was much more like me when it came to wanting the best out of life. But I was never prepared to walk away. Not only did I really love Kenny, but he was still the popular college football star who got invited to all kinds of top-shelf events as a keynote speaker. Those engagements brought in some loot, and if I helped him work it, that could still be our ticket. But it was going to take some time for that river to start flowing, which is why I'd kept my gig at Foxtails even after I graduated. Dancing for and dating the men at the club gave me the money that Kenny couldn't provide...yet. And not only money, but other gifts of gratitude: diamonds, gold, and fur. It was all the same. All good to me.

It wasn't too hard to keep that side of my life from Kenny. He wasn't looking for anything; he never expected my deception, so he never saw it. Plus, I had an arsenal of lies that were easy for my husband-to-be to believe. From the non-existent humongous insurance policy that my mother supposedly left me and my sister, to the late hours I had to keep because that was the best way for a newly-hired assistant Marketing Director like me to make the best impression and begin her climb up the corporate ladder. My lies kept my life in order.

But the thing was, I didn't want to start off my marriage as a liar. So as I eased my way up the front steps of Foxtails, I promised myself that no matter what Buck had to say, this would be the very last time that I stepped inside this place.

I swung the heavy front door open and just like the first time I'd entered this club, darkness and music hit me. It was just ten in the morning, and the club didn't officially open 'til noon, but still Buck always kept the music blasting just in case an early customer walked in. I paused for a moment, the familiar feeling of power almost overtaking me. But then I moved forward, trying my best to stay focused on my future while I left behind all memories of my past.

I took just a few steps to my left and found Buck where he always seemed to be: behind the bar.

"What's up?"

Buck swung his almost three-hundred pound frame around and grinned. "'Sup with you? You coming back?"

"I don't have any time for this." I folded my arms. "Either you tell me what this is about or I'm outta here."

"Dang. What's your hurry? I thought you'd want to hang out for a little while, slide down a pole or two, you know, for old times' sake."

"Buck!"

"All right. Geez." He took a swig from the bottle he was holding.

I shook my head. Buck was drinking beer like it was orange juice.

He said, "There's someone here to see you."

My eyes narrowed because though Buck protected me, I didn't have anyone to protect me from him. "Who?"

Buck shrugged. "He asked me not to tell you."

"More games?"

Buck held up his hands. "Hey, I don't have anything to do with this one. He said to just tell you to come on back."

My old boss didn't have to tell me where "come on back" was. I was even more annoyed now. For all I knew, Buck could've been setting me up – he could've had someone in the back waiting to get down with me. But my inquiring mind needed to know what this mystery was about. I frowned at Buck, just to let him know again how pissed I was, and then sauntered toward the red velvet curtains, to a room that I'd grown to both love and hate.

When I first became a dancer, I prided myself on the fact that I truly only danced. I wasn't like the other girls who were doing far more than stripping.

But then I met Mr. Smith. All of his money, and all of his gifts changed everything. And though I danced for that white man privately and lay with him unashamedly, I only had sex with Mr. Smith once...for six thousand dollars on his last night in Los Angeles.

That six thousand dollars opened the door and took my...dancing...to a whole 'nother level. Once the door was open, I couldn't find a way to close it – not until three months ago.

Now, as I stood outside the room that had given me so much physical pleasure and psychological pain, I wondered not only who was on the other side, but who did I wanted it to be. There were hundreds of men who'd made my sexual acquaintance over the four years of my dancing career, but I didn't have a clue which one had summoned me here.

Stepping inside, I waited a moment for my eyes to adjust to the dimmed light. And then I saw him.

"What's up, sweetheart?"

I smiled and walked right into his waiting arms.

"Hines! What are you doing here?"

He kissed my forehead, sat down on the velvet love seat, then reached for my hand to pull me down next to him. We snuggled, though we didn't do it on purpose. It was the way the soft velvet love seats were designed – like bean bag chairs – our bodies didn't have any choice but to kinda meld together.

Not that I minded. Hines was one of my best "dates," sexually and monetarily. And if he'd called me here to Foxtails to get down, then I would just have to give up my quest to be a virtuous woman on my wedding day. Because right about now, I could use a piece of this man.

"What are you doing here?" I asked. "I didn't even know you were in L.A."

He leaned back and unbuttoned the jacket of what I was sure was at least an eight-hundred dollar suit. He put his arm around me. "I'm still moving around, from here to there."

"So, no more football at all? Ever?"

He shook his head. "They were serious when they kicked me out the league," he said, as if it was no big deal that he'd lost his multi-million dollar contract with the Los Angeles Raiders. "I'm banned for life."

It may not have been a big deal to Hines, but it was major to all the football fans who'd been thrilled beyond measure when the Oakland Raiders had deserted the North and migrated to the South, bringing their star rookie running back with them. Hines Gifford was a sensation who had broken all kind of records at Florida State and was expected to do the same with the Raiders. The talk on the street was that the Raiders wanted Hines so bad that when he said he would only play if he could be in L.A., they moved the entire franchise. It had been hard for people to believe that one player – a rookie at that – could have that kind of pull. I didn't believe any of that myself, until Hines and his boys had come into Foxtails one night.

Foxtails was known as a place where the big spenders liked to drop their dollars, so I was used to the kind of money that Hines was tossing around. But it was what was beyond the money that impressed me. Hines had a confidence that was definite, but not cocky; a strut that was self assured, but not prideful. It was just clear that he knew what he wanted, and whatever he wanted, he was gonna get.

Then, in Hines's second year, the news came out that he was involved in some major league trouble.

I said, "I still can't believe that anyone would really think that you were in the mafia. I mean, what kind of proof did they have?" I only asked that question because I was in a curious mood and really wanted to know if Hines was going to confirm anything or deny everything. Not that I needed him to say a word; I'd pretty much made up my mind, like the millions of other people in this country. Hines Gifford was all up in that mess. He'd been linked to the Adamo family, second only to the Gottis in organized crime. According to all the stuff I'd read in the *Star* and *National Enquirer*, even while Hines was playing football, he and his boys were running the mafia's L.A. sports operations, everything from scalping tickets to shaving points. And it was rumored that he had "taken care" of a few people here and a few people there when he received orders from the Adamos to do so.

The rumors and accusations were rampant; no one knew what was fact or what was fiction. Then suddenly at the beginning of Hines's third year, he was cut from the Raiders. The thing that was so heavy, though, was that they were still going to pay him his contract, which was unheard of in the NFL. It was the lead story on every channel, on the front page of every newspaper, and on the tongue of every DJ. It was nothing but a thrilling mess.

Hines said, "I didn't come down here to talk about all my troubles."

"You don't look like you got any troubles." I let my eyes roll over all of his Denzel-esque fineness. I wasn't going to initiate it, but all he had to do was ask me once and my panties would be gone.

He chuckled. "Trust me, I got a-plenty. But today, sweetheart, it's all about you." I took a breath; I was ready to stand up and pull my dress down. "Buck tells me you're getting married."

It had been at least a year since I'd seen Hines, but the thing was, I'd been engaged to Kenny for a year and a half. "You knew that I was going to do that."

His nod was slow and steady and his eyes bore into mine like he was studying me hard, making my temperature rise. "So, you're really gonna marry the ol' dude?"

"Yeah," I said, as if he should have known that I was going to keep my word.

Hines wasn't the only one of my "dates" who knew about Kenny. I'd read once in *Essence* magazine that when a man cheated, he never told the woman he loved about 'the others,' but 'the others' always knew about the one he loved, as if secrets were only kept from those you cared about. It seemed like twisted logic to me, but hey, it was from *Essence* so I went along with it, figuring that the same equation should work for women.

So everyone knew about Kenny...and Kenny knew about no one. My proof that he was my one and only. The men I danced for and dated may have had their hands on my body, but Kenny held my heart.

I said to Hines, "I told you a long time ago that I was in love with Kenny."

Hines did his slow nod once again as his eyes became clearer, like he was finally believing me.

"So, this is why you came down here? Just to ask if I was really getting married?" I was pissed with myself for letting my mind take me to that other place. Hines didn't want to sleep with me, and now I was going to have to find a way to dispose of all this sexual stress he'd built up in me.

"Yeah," he said. "To ask you that and to give you this." He slipped his hand inside his jacket and pulled out a black velvet box. "This is for you, sweetheart. Sort of a congratulations, going-away present."

His words gave me chills and sent a thrill through my body. Hines had given me lots of gifts over the years that I'd known him, but a girl never got tired of getting something new. When Hines flipped back the top of the box, my eyes got as big as the diamond that shined in front of me. I hadn't seen a ring this beautiful since Princess Diana's engagement to Prince Charles a few years back.

"What is this?" I whispered, as if I couldn't tell it was a ring.

Without a word, he lifted my left hand and glanced down at the engagement ring that I wore. For a moment, I wanted to snatch back my hand and hide what was on my ring finger. But then, I lifted my hand higher, like I was proud of the diamond chip that Kenny had given me.

I was proud. My baby had done the best he could. And once we were married and I was really able to get him moving in his career, I would be getting an upgrade – believe that.

But my pride didn't mean a thing to Hines. He chuckled, then before I could say anything, slipped the chip off my finger and replaced it with the rock.

"What are you doing?" I asked, raising my voice. Even though I had lots of questions, it wasn't like I tried to stop him, though. I just let him put that ring on my finger.

He laughed. "Don't trip, Pepper," he said, calling me by my stage name. "I'm not trying to marry you. I ain't that kind of cat."

Well, I didn't want to marry him either. Not really. "So what's up with this ring?" He kissed my forehead. "Like I said, it's a good-bye gift for the best dancer...and date...this side of the moon."

I glanced back at the ring. It was beginning to feel heavy (it had to be at least four carats) on my finger.

There was no way that I could keep this, could I? I mean, what was I supposed to tell Kenny?

As if Hines could hear the questions turning over in my mind, he said, "I don't expect you to wear it. This is just something special between you and me. Just to make sure that you'll never forget me, 'cause I'm sure 'nuff always gonna remember you." He tucked the junior achievement ring Kenny had given me into the palm of my hand and stood up.

"I gotta go, sweetheart. Gotta make things happen."

I was still kinda frozen in place, weighed down by the ring and my thoughts. I didn't move until Hines took my hand and lifted me from the couch. He held me in a hug for just a moment, and then flicked a card between his fingers. "I just want you to know that I'll always be here for you. If you ever need me, if that man doesn't treat you right, call me."

He pressed the card into the palm of my hand. I watched him strut out the back door, the private entrance and exit for the biggest and most discreet celebrities. I stood alone and looked down at Kenny's ring in one hand and Hines' card in the other, then spread my fingers to appreciate the diamond that Hines had given me.

It was a shame I would have to hide this ring away, but I didn't have to do that right now, did I? I mean, I wasn't getting married until tomorrow and no one was gonna see me today. And really, what would it hurt to wear this for just a few hours? I still loved Kenny, I was still going to marry him. Wearing this ring would be a whole lotta fun for a little while.

I couldn't do anything except smile as I tucked Kenny's ring and Hines' card inside the pocket of my purse. Then I did my own strut out the VIP door.

Chapter 4

My temperature was rising, and it had very little to do with the ninety-degree heat wave we were having. So I paid five dollars to park my car just feet away from the ocean and strolled along the Venice beach boardwalk. I needed to cool off – in every way – and sport this ring on my left hand for at least a few hours. The walkway was thick with Los Angelenos even though today was Friday. Friday, in any other part of the country was a weekday, meaning that it was a workday. But not in the place I called home. In L.A., weekends began on Thursday, sometimes even Wednesday evenings. So today was just another weekend in August in Venice, California.

Cheers rose in the air as I passed the paddle tennis court where two couples competed, dressed in typical – at least for L.A. – paddle tennis attire: bikinis for the women and Speedos for the guys. No matter how many times I saw this sight, I still had to shake my head. Yes, I took off my clothes for a living, but you were not about to find me jiggling all up and down anybody's court, giving a show for free.

I strolled past the shops where T-shirts sold three for five dollars, and tattoo shop owners shouted to all who passed by about the glorious benefits of having ink blazed into your skin. On the other side, a crowd gathered around a steel band. Just feet away from that show was the guy who juggled a tennis ball, a bowling ball and a chainsaw like it was nothing.

I ignored it all. I didn't come down here to be entertained. My purpose was to cool off and calm down before I headed to the hotel. Then, I was going to luxuriate – yes, luxuriate – for the rest of the afternoon and into the night in the splendor of the new Ritz Carlton hotel.

It had been my idea to have our wedding at the Ritz. I just couldn't see getting married in a church. It was more than my past that made me want to stay clear of any altar; I just didn't have any kind of relationship with any church. I'd only been in a church once since my mom's funeral, and that was only because Kyla made me stand up for her at her wedding. I didn't see any reason to hang out in God's house after He'd let me down and taken my mother away.

Of course, my father and Kyla weren't happy with the fact that I would be exchanging vows before a judge instead of God. Both of them had tried to get me to agree to let their pastor officiate. But I wasn't feeling that Jheri curl-sporting, leisure-suit wearing Pastor Davis my father loved so much. Especially not after I saw him one night in Foxtails tossing dollars on the stage faster than anyone else. Pastor Davis saw me, too, though he ducked out of the club right after we made eye contact. But I wasn't worried about him slithering away and saying anything. If he kept his mouth shut, I would too. Of course he sealed his lips; he had far more to lose than I did.

Then Kyla's pastor, Pastor Ford...well, that lady just gave me the heebie-jeebies. Whenever I saw her, she always greeted me with kindness and a smile, but she would hold my hand and then look at me like she was seeing right through to my soul. Sometimes I wondered if God was telling her all my business. And if she did have it like that with God, then, I didn't want to stand before her...or Him.

Standing before the judge would be just fine.

I'd chosen the Ritz Carlton for one other reason, too: it was the only way to at least keep up a little with Kyla and Jefferson's wedding. Theirs was an extravaganza that didn't make any kind of sense. First, they had packed the church to standing room only, and then the Carringtons had rented out one of the biggest yachts in the marina and the two hundred and fifty guests sailed and ate and drank and danced the night away as we floated on the peninsula.

It was a celebration that – I hate to admit – had made me jealous. Don't get me wrong, I loved me some Kyla Carrington Blake. But it was hard not to feel just a little bit of envy toward her and the way she'd grown up, and all the money that her parents had. I had to have a wedding that didn't make me feel inferior.

Of course, there weren't going to be as many attending my wedding, and my guests were going to keep their feet on dry land, but I was determined to have my fifty guests *oohing* and *ahhing*. This wedding was costing me a small fortune: from my designer dress, to the bridal suite for the weekend, to the ceremony and the reception on the Ballroom Terrace of the Ritz, I was spending close to seven thousand dollars. It was the last of the money that I'd had from my days at Foxtails. But that was cool. In a way, I felt good about that. Not good about starting off my marriage broke, but good that there would be no Foxtails money between me and Kenny once we exchanged our vows.

And though my bank account would be empty after this weekend, I would still have a few things to hold onto. Gifts, mostly jewelry. Especially this ring. The Foxtails men had set me up; it would be a long time before I'd be broke-broke.

I held my hand out straight in front of me and the sun beamed down on the clear stone, making every color of the rainbow dance across my fingers. This oval cut diamond had to be one of the prettiest rings I'd ever seen.

"Jasmine!"

Turning to where the shout had come from, I saw the next best thing to this ring: a fine looking man. It took me a moment to realize where I was – right in front of the real reason for my trip to the beach. Yeah, I could deny it, but I wasn't into lying. At least not to myself. I knew exactly who and what I wanted to see when I'd made that left turn on Venice Boulevard and headed toward the ocean.

But even with those thoughts in my mind, I widened my eyes like I was surprised.

"Roman?" I said his name as though he was some kind of apparition I couldn't believe that I was seeing. I stepped onto the grass, moving closer to the weight pen known as Muscle Beach.

Roman sat on the edge of a bench, his biceps bulging as he held a barbell. But even though he was my focus, my eyes wandered to the others who were lifting weights behind him. There was nothing but hard bodies, muscled bodies, sculpted bodies, gorgeous bodies. All of those men, black, brown, yellow, and white, it didn't matter - they were all fine as the high noon sun glistened and moistened their skin. It was a woman's paradise.

But my eyes didn't linger. I turned my gaze back to the one who really had my attention.

Mr. Chocolate grinned as he secured the weight back on the stand, then strolled to the side so that the two of us could be up close and personal.

"What's up?" he said.

"Just you."

"I see you decided to accept my invitation and come on down to see me."

"No. I was just strolling on the beach and forgot that you worked down here."

He chuckled as if he knew I was a liar. "So," he finally said, "where's your husband?"

"I'm not married yet."

Now he laughed outright, as if I'd told a joke. That pissed me off. "Don't worry, you'll get to meet him," I said, as if that was a threat. "Once we're married, I'll bring him down here."

"Why isn't he with you now?"

"'Cause he's a working man." I paused and looked Roman up and down. "And, since he had to work today, I decided to take a stroll."

"Oh, okay," he said and laughed some more.

What was up with that? Was he laughing at me? He didn't need to get all cocky about anything. It wasn't like I was chasing him. "No, really, I just came down here to cool off."

"Is that what you call it?"

Oh, see, now he was trying to play me. That was fine; he was making this easy. I was just gonna take my butt straight over to that hotel. There was plenty of air-conditioning at the Ritz. "Well, you have a good workout," I said, already walking away. I curled my fingers into a wave and turned my back on him.

"Wait! Wait! Jasmine, wait!" he yelled after me.

But I kept on walking. In less than a minute, though, Mr. Chocolate was by my side.

"Didn't you hear me calling you?" he said, though I could hear the laughter inside his voice.

"I didn't hear a thing," I responded, not even looking at him.

"Come on, now. Don't be like that. I was just playing."

I still didn't say a word. Just kept on walking. And he kept up with me.

"It was just a joke. I was just glad to see you, that's all. I'm sorry...maybe I said the wrong thing."

I stopped, and glared him down the way only a soul sista could. "Yeah, you did," I said, giving him major attitude.

"I'm sorry."

I crossed my arms and pursed my lips.

"What?" he said, shrugging a little. "You don't believe in forgiveness?"

"Oh, I believe in it all right."

"Then," he said, and took a step closer. It was hard to do, since we were already almost pressed together by the masses strolling past us. "Then, please forgive me."

He was back to using that voice he'd used to capture me last night. His stage voice, the one that was meant to get a woman to drop her panties. And his eyes...those green eyes.

"Do you forgive me?" he asked. His bottom lip quivered, but not in the way it would if he'd been upset. No, this was more like a hypnotist's trick – getting me to stare so long and so hard at his lip that all I wanted to do was gently suck it between my teeth. I had to fight to keep my balance, to keep my reason. "All right," I said, kind of shyly, though I had no idea why that sweet, soft sound came out of me. This was not my personality.

"Great." He stepped back a bit, giving me room to breathe. "So, do you want some company while you...stroll?"

"No. I don't wanna disturb your workout."

"Oh, I'm done," he said. "I'm ready to move on to new things."

I paused, wondering what he meant. Did it matter? There was nothing wrong with innocent flirting. And wasn't this exactly what I wanted? An outlet for all that was bubbling inside?

"Just give me a couple of moments," he said as he walked back toward the weight pen. I followed. "Let me get my things."

He trotted in front of me, and all my eyes could do was watch his butt. Dang! Bang! It! That man was fine in ways that had yet to be defined!

It didn't take long for Roman to come out with a gym bag hanging from his shoulder. "Lead the way," he said and motioned with his hand.

We walked side-by-side, pressing through the crowd, past the skateboarders and roller skaters and tourists who stopped every five steps to take in the sights. One of those sights was Roman himself. I noticed the way so many people glanced our way. I knew what it was: Roman and I were a beautiful couple. But if I was honest – and like I said, I always was with myself – it was really Roman who was getting all the attention. Women, and a whole lot of men, couldn't help staring at him.

I wasn't intimidated or insecure about that, though. I loved the feeling of being with this man. We continued to walk, not speaking, not stopping, just strolling, so comfortable in each other's presence. As if we were meant to be.

In front of the Sidewalk Cafe, Roman said, "Have you eaten yet?" I shook my head, and he led me to the long line that twisted around the side of the restaurant.

"You want to eat here?" I asked. I'd been coming to Venice beach since I was a kid, and I'd never had lunch at this eatery. The line was always way too long for me to waste my time just for a hamburger. "We won't get in for an hour!"

"Stay right here," he whispered. He disappeared into the café, and in less than a minute, he was back, gesturing for me to join him at the front of the line. Taking my hand, he led me past all of the waiting people. The hostess grinned at Roman until she saw me. With a scowl, she led us to a premier table on the edge of the boardwalk. But before we could sit down, a woman sitting at the table next to ours jumped up.

"Roman!" she exclaimed.

"Hey, Sheri, what's up?" As Roman stepped forward to hug the woman, she took two giant steps back, knocking over her chair in the process.

Without another word to Roman, the woman grabbed her purse from the table and turned to the guy who was with her. "I'll wait for you outside," she said. She hadn't even finished speaking before she tore out of there like she was being chased by a killer.

I frowned. The man at the table frowned.

And Roman grinned. He shrugged, then turned his attention back to me and the hostess who had watched the whole exchange.

When we finally sat down, the hostess handed Roman his menu, then she tossed mine across the table to me.

"What was that about?" I asked the moment we were alone.

"What? Lisa?" He shook his head. "Don't pay her any attention. She acts like that whenever I come here. She just wants me."

I leaned back and raised one eyebrow. This man sure was cocky. "I'm talking about the girl who ran out of here. Who took one look at you and cut like she owed you some money or something."

That made him laugh. "Sheri's just a girl I used to know back in the day."

Glancing at my menu, I said, "Seems like she doesn't want to know you now."

"I guess she's still upset because I broke off the little thing we had going." He sighed. "She was hurt when we broke up, but there wasn't any point in continuing something that wasn't going anywhere."

"That's all it was?"

"What else could it be?"

I nodded and turned my eyes back to my menu. Yeah, it was clear that Sheri was a jilted lover, and that made me wonder how many hearts this man had broken.

"So, you really eat this kind of stuff?" I asked, wanting to change the subject.

"What stuff? Food?" He laughed and I joined him.

"It's just that the way you look...."

He rested his arms on the table, then leaned toward me. "I'm so glad that you noticed."

I don't know why, but I felt like I was blushing. I couldn't remember that feeling...ever! I looked down at the menu, needing a moment to get myself together. I was Jasmine Cox. I didn't fawn over men...men fawned over me.

So, I came back with, "Yeah, I noticed. And with the way you look, I didn't think a morsel of food ever crossed your lips."

"More than food has crossed these lips, baby."

"Oh, please." I waved my hand as if I was totally unimpressed with his flirtation, even though I was disturbed by it a little, and loving it a lot. "So," I said, "what's good here?"

"Don't tell me this is your first time...." I looked up and he finished, "here."

His bottom lip trembled again, and I had such a hard time breaking my eyes away. I forced my gaze upward, but staring into his eyes was no better. Those green eyes were piercing and he stared as if he was trying to get me to look away first.

But he didn't know that he'd met his match.

I said, "Yeah, this is my first time...here. I'm a virgin, I guess you could say."

"A virgin, really?"

"Yeah," I nodded. "Ever had one of those?"

The shock of my words pushed him back against his chair.

I laughed. "I'm talking about...." I paused and picked up the drink menu that had been stuffed between the salt and pepper shakers. "I'm talking about one of these. A virgin Pina Colada."

He blinked. "That's not what you were talking about."

"Yes, it was. I was talking about a drink." I placed the menu back in its place. "I can't help it if your mind went somewhere else."

"And I can't help it either, since you were the one who took me there."

"Did I?" I tilted my head, but I leaned away from him. This flirtation was helping to quash my rising stress. But still I needed to pull this conversation back to safer ground. This was fun, but it was dangerous...especially since I found this green-eye chocolate bar so delicious.

A sun-kissed waiter (who looked like the type who told everyone who asked that he was an actor) jotted down our orders. Once he left us alone, I said, "So tell me about Roman." I took a sip of my water. I needed something to cool me off, to cool me down.

"I'd rather talk about Jasmine."

"What do you want to know about me?"

"Everything."

"That could take a lot of time."

He shrugged. "We got all day...and all night."

That was an invitation that I so wished that I could accept. Just by looking at him, I knew what it would be like to be with him. I could already feel Roman on me, over me, in me.

I squeezed my knees together, sipped more water and said the right thing: "Did you forget I'm getting married in the morning?"

"Nope," he said. "You keep telling me that over and over, so how could I forget?"

"I just want to make sure that you remember."

"I remember, but that has nothing to do with me."

My surprise had to be all over my face.

He said, "All I'm trying to do is get to know you better."

"For what purpose?"

"For friendly purposes."

I laughed. "That was funny." I raised my glass in a toast to him. "But you know that's not possible. We can't be friends."

"Because you're getting married."

"Right."

"And because you would never cheat on your husband."

"Right again."

"Okay, I got it, I get it, but can you do me a favor?" The question was rhetorical because he didn't even take a breath. "There are a lot of hours between now and tomorrow. So can we just forget about what's gonna happen in the morning?"

Before the question was completely out of his mouth, his hand was over mine, and the spark that surged through me gave me such a jolt that I jerked my hand away, though he didn't seem to notice.

He said, "Now that we're forgetting about tomorrow, we can have a good time today. So, can you please tell me all about Jasmine?"

I was hardly forgetting about tomorrow, but I went along with his question. Over my salad and his protein burger, I gave him the vital statistics only – that I'd been born and raised in L.A., that I'd gone to school in Inglewood, that I worked at Carnation, and that I hoped to one day leave the Golden State. Then, before it got too personal, I turned the tables, and he told me all about his dreams to open up a string of fitness clubs. That's why he danced: because it was good exercise, because the tips were more than he could make anywhere else, and because he could hand out his cards to let women know about his future business.

"You didn't give me your card last night," I said.

Roman pushed his plate aside. "That's because I wanted to give you so much more." This man was coming at me hard, with his words, his touch...and his lips. Those mesmerizing lips.

I needed to change the subject. "Okay, so besides working out and planning your business, what do you like to do?"

"My favorite way to spend an afternoon...is horizontally."

I laughed, but it was definitely time – time to cut and run. Because the truth was that if I stayed any longer, whatever he was selling, I was gonna buy.

I glanced at my watch. "It's getting late."

"Okay, where to now?"

I looked him dead in his eyes. "I'm going to the hotel."

"Not home?"

"I'm staying at the Ritz tonight. That's where the wedding will be tomorrow."

"I've never been to the Ritz."

I chuckled. As if he could get me with that little hint. Like I was supposed to invite him to the hotel just to check out the room. Yeah, right.

Roman raised his hand in the air, motioned for the waiter, then pulled his wallet from his bag. When I reached for my own wallet, he shook his head.

"Your money's no good here," he said. This was hardly a five-star restaurant; the bill couldn't have been more than twenty dollars, but I appreciated the sentiment. Still, it was definitely time for me to move on before those lips and those eyes and that glistening bald head got to me even more.

The crowd had thinned as the day edged toward evening, and the walk back to my car was much faster. Like he'd done last night, Roman opened the door for me. For a moment, I hesitated, expecting so much more from him. Surely, he was going to make a move.

But he did nothing. And I was glad about it. I think.

"So," I said wanting to give him one more moment. When he didn't say anything, I slipped into the car.

He closed the door, then waited for me to roll down the window before he leaned inside. "Thank you for spending your last hours as a single woman with me."

I couldn't remember a time when I'd been more proud of myself. I mean, here was this man, with all of his magnificence right in front of my face. His lips were so close that a mere movement would have connected us and it wasn't hard to imagine all the ways that those lips could satisfy me.

The familiar heat smoldered between my legs and I revved up the BMW's engine.

"Thank you," he repeated, as if he wanted me to respond.

But I had nothing more than a wave for him. He backed away and I pulled out, stunned that I was really letting this man go. Slowly, I maneuvered through the lot, putting distance between me and temptation. But, my eyes stayed on the rear-view mirror and the view of Roman...and I remembered him as he was last night – in that fireman's ensemble.

That was when my heat flickered into flames.

"Keep driving," I whispered to myself, and pressed the A/C button on the dashboard, adjusted the vents and blasted that cold air right onto my face.

"I'm doing the right thing," I said.

But though the air blew cold, I was fire hot. I couldn't stop the blaze that burned and quickly spread through me. It was a wildfire; it was sexual combustion. There was nothing that I could do.

I slammed on the brakes, pushed the car into reverse, and skidded back to where my satisfaction stood.

With a smile and without a word, Roman hopped in. As much as I wanted to wait for Kenny to take care of me tomorrow, I needed Roman to put out this fire tonight.

I pressed the accelerator to the floor and headed toward the Ritz Carlton Hotel.

Chapter 5

This was the life I needed to live.

I needed to wake up every day just like this on the softest silk sheets known to man, surrounded by the elegance of this Victorian decor, with the marina right outside my window. I felt rich, I felt sexy, I felt satisfied in the luxury of this bridal suite; I wanted to live like this always, forever a bride.

Rolling over, I smiled at the round mound of chocolate next to me – and that was just his head because round was not the way I would've described any other part of him. This man was all muscles: a lean, mean, male machine.

So here I was in this bridal suite, not yet a bride, lying next to the man who was not my husband to be. But who could blame me? How could I not take advantage of the opportunity that was handed to me to live out this ecstasy-filled fantasy?

And ecstasy-filled it was! Last night had been nothing but pure pleasure. Roman was my favorite kind of lover; the time we spent together had been all about me. His hands explored, his tongue wandered, and he had me singing in twenty-seven different languages – all at once – while he carried me around the suite with my legs clinging to his waist. Then, when I introduced him to my favorite position – upside down – I had him singing, too. Roman wanted to go all night, and I'm telling you, there's nothing like a man who is ready and willing to do the bidding of a sex-starved woman.

Roman's skills had me all messed up. He made me forget all about my plan, which was to just bring him back here to the hotel for an hour or two. I planned to send him home before dark, sure that by then he would have scratched my three-week itch. But how was I supposed to know then that I'd given this man the appropriate nickname – Mr. Chocolate. He was as addictive as any Godiva bar. And that was why two hours had turned into four, then eight, and now it was almost six in the morning and the sun was rising on my wedding day.

It was definitely time to let this man go.

I gave Roman a shove, but when he didn't move, I pushed harder. I hoped he wasn't going to be one of those hard-to-wake-up dudes. I needed this man up and out of this room. Not only did I need to put some time and space between this mistake and my future, but I needed him gone before I got busted. Kyla wasn't coming over until seven, but knowing my best friend, her promptness and excitement might have her knocking on this door much earlier. Not to mention my sister, Serena – and the wedding planner, Yolanda, who had been assigned to me by the hotel. It wouldn't do me well to have any of those people see me with a man who didn't look anything like my husband to be.

"It's time to get up," I said when Roman stirred just a bit.

He rolled over and his eyes opened slowly. Then, he grinned and stretched, kicking the sheet off at the same time.

I looked down at his body and sighed.

He said, "Morning, sunshine."

The look that he gave me – like he wanted more – and the look I gave his body – like I wanted more – had me longing to fall right into his arms. But I had to stop this madness and start acting like the bride-to-be that I was.

Roman reached for me and with all the strength I had, I pushed his hands away.

"Sorry. Can't do that anymore," I said, as lightly as I could.

"What? Don't you believe in morning love?"

I chuckled. "Trust me, I do. It's just that I can't do morning love with you."

"Why not?"

"First of all, I don't have time. And secondly, I'm not about to have sex with anyone but my husband on my wedding day."

He laughed, hard, like I'd just told a Saturday Night Live kinda joke. "Oh, so having sex with someone besides your husband the night before your wedding is cool?"

Roman had me there. I mean, I really did feel horrible about what had gone down last night, but what was I supposed to do? I was a woman who was used to getting mine on a regular basis. Having lots of sex and having lots of good sex. The sex part, I could get from Kenny. But the good sex part…not so much. Not that it was Kenny's fault. He had no idea that he was competing with all of these men in my mind.

I sighed. My goal really and truly had been to stay celibate (for three weeks) so that my first night as Kenny Larson's wife would be really special. But maybe all was not lost. Maybe it would still be great with Kenny because *we* hadn't been together in such a long time. And maybe once Kenny and I took these vows, my body would catch up with my heart and I would be satisfied the way I'd been satisfied with him throughout high school and three years of college. The way I'd been satisfied before I began working at Foxtails and discovering sex on a whole 'nother level.

Finally I said to Roman, "Sleeping with you last night was unfortunate." I made it sound like I'd just made a little mistake. "I shouldn't have done it, but stuff happens, you know?"

He smirked. "Stuff?"

"Yup, stuff. Good stuff, I'll admit that. But, wrong stuff."

His eyebrows rose so high, I was sure they were going to slip off his forehead.

"Look," I said, "there's nothing I can do about what happened. I don't look back and I don't live with regrets. So, all I'll say is that I had a great time with you, but now it's over...bye-bye!"

He chuckled as if he didn't believe I had enough will power to really walk away from what he had laid on me. But he just didn't know. I was Jasmine Cox-about-to-be-Larson. I could walk away from him or anyone or anything. 'Cause I was the one who was always in control.

I rolled off the bed and strutted to the dresser, not caring at all that I was butt-naked. My mind was already on the events that were going to go down over the next few hours. Glancing in the mirror, I twisted my head from side to side, taking in the damage I'd done from a night of hard sex and then sleeping without my silk scarf. My asymmetrical hair cut was matted flat against my head, making me look nothing like a bride. Kyla was gonna kill me, but that was fine. All she was gonna do was fuss and then fix me up. By noon, I'd be ready to walk down the aisle looking like the most beautiful blushing bride.

The blushing part made me look beyond my reflection in the mirror and glance at Roman. He was still in the bed · with his elbow cocked, and his head resting in the palm of his hand – as if my goodbye speech had not moved him. Literally. He just stared at me, his eyes glazed with appreciation. As if I was a valuable piece of art, like a black Mona Lisa or something.

"You know, you're one fine female."

I pivoted around so that Roman could get a full frontal view of all of my glory. Foxtails had been such a great breeding ground for my self-esteem. It was there that I learned the power of a woman. And it was moments like this when I felt almighty. Because without doing anything more than showing the body that had made me lots of money, I could bring a grown man to his knees. I could make a grown man cry. I could turn a grown man into a babbling, begging buffoon.

"Yup," he said, with eyes that were even more glassy now. "Fine."

"Thank you."

"I sure wish I could get another piece of that today."

Slowly, I strolled toward him. There wasn't much on my body that jiggled, but what was supposed to did.

And Roman did what all men did when they saw me like this: he licked his lips and began to pant, and that meant the begging, babbling part wasn't very far away.

But I was just teasing. He was never going to get another piece of me. All I was doing now was gifting him with a sight to remember me by.

I stood over the bed and looked down at him. "Sorry, boo. No seconds here. This was just a one-time thing."

"Don't be so sure."

"Oh, I'm sure."

"Well what would you say if I told you that this isn't over until I said it was over?"

This time, it was my eyebrows that rose high. Roman was still smiling, but that didn't mean a thing. Just as I was about to start cursing this man out, he chuckled.

"I was just playing," he said.

It was my turn to stare at him, but I wasn't looking at him with the appreciation that had been in his eyes when he looked at me. I was trying to see inside his head. Please don't tell me that I had hooked up with a crazy!

But as soon as I had that thought, Roman laughed. "I said, I was just playing. I knew what this was when I walked into this room with you yesterday. Just a one-time thing. I didn't even think that you'd let me stay the night, but I'm glad you did because I really did have a good time."

I wasn't sure if he was lying or not, but I kinda figured that those words deserved, if not a reward, a peace offering. If this guy was crazy, I didn't want to piss him off. I just wanted to get him out of here and make sure that we parted – at least in his mind – as friends.

So, I leaned over and kissed him, letting my tongue say a slow goodbye. But when his hands began to roam over my body, and goose bumps rose on my skin, and he brought back those last-night memories, I started having second thoughts. It might be good to give him a quickie...I had time...it could be short and sweet...what would it matter?

But I pushed him away because it would matter. It would matter because today was my wedding day. And no matter what anyone thought, I *did* have morals!

I rolled off the bed, then glanced at Roman over my shoulder. "I'm going into the bathroom," I said. "When I come out, please be gone."

His face stretched with surprise and his expression told me that he found my words a bit abrasive. I was sorry for that – my tone was harsher than my heart. But if that's what was needed to make him be gone, then fine. I had to keep my mind on what was important here, and that was getting him out of the room so that I could prepare to become Kenny's bride.

I went into the bathroom, lowered the cover on the commode, sat down and waited. For a while, I was sure that he was going to knock on the door and ask to use the toilet. Isn't that what everyone did in the morning?

I folded my hands together and that was when I saw it – the ring! Dang! I'd forgotten that I still had on Hines's ring. Can you imagine what would have happened if I walked into the church wearing this?

Jumping up from the toilet, I put my ear to the door. There was nothing. Still, I waited just a bit longer, just in case, before I stepped into the bedroom.

It was empty.

The only sign that Roman had been there were the tousled sheets and rumpled comforter that had been tossed onto the floor some time during the middle of the night.

I strolled through the grand bedroom and into the even grander living room. There was no sign of Roman, but I noticed an undershirt draped over the arm of the sofa. It took me a moment to figure out what it was and when I lifted it up, I laughed.

Call me any time, and call me often! That's what Roman had scribbled across the shirt that he'd left behind for me. Was he kidding? Shaking my head, I folded the shirt and took it with me into the bedroom. I was never going to call him. Last night was last night. And now it was over.

I stepped inside the walk-in closet, stuffed Roman's shirt into the bottom of my bag, then slid off Hines's ring. I kissed that big ol' diamond goodbye before I tucked it into my purse and slipped my real ring back onto my finger. This was okay – soon my boo would be able to afford the best for me.

Turning to my wedding dress, I gently pulled it off the hanger and cradled it like a baby in my arms before I laid it atop of the disheveled sheets of the bridal bed. Stepping back, I studied the Barber original. The purity that the designer had captured in that gown did not belong anywhere near the decadence that had gone down on that mattress over the last few hours.

So, I gathered the dress once again, and carried it into the living room. Roman and I had spent a couple of hours in this part of the suite, but most of the time, I was pinned up against the balcony windows. The couch was virgin territory. Gently, I spread out the satin dress over the sofa, then stepped back.

That was better.

It was the quiet and the gown and the opulence all around me that made me realize what I was about to do. The realization weighed heavy on my shoulders and I had to ask myself, did I really want to do this? Staring at the dress, I asked that question over and over.

"Yes," I said aloud. "I want to be Mrs. Kenny Larson."

I had wanted to be this man's wife for a long time now, and there had to be a reason why we'd lasted all of these years. We were meant to be and with just a little help, Kenny would become the provider. He would become the husband that I needed. I had no doubt that he would work hard on that. And in return, I would work hard on becoming the best wife I could be. I knew I would make that promise to him in just a few hours, but I made it to myself right then. This was my solemn vow.

That pledge made me feel even worse about what I'd done last night, but those blissful hours were in the past, right? Never to be revisited. I could start anew. I could be a good wife; after all, it was in my DNA. My mother had been the perfect wife – dutiful, faithful, respectful – until the day she died. I could be all of that.

The knock on the door drew me away from my thoughts and I scurried to the closet first, slipping into a bathrobe. By the time I got to the door, the knock had come again. Glancing at the grandfather clock, I was glad that I knew my friend so well. It was just a little past six-thirty and Roman had barely been gone fifteen minutes.

"Jasmine!" Kyla squealed, as if she hadn't seen me in years.

"You're early," I said and hugged her – but then my eyes opened wide and my mouth clamped shut.

When Kyla saw me looking over her shoulder, she said, "Oh, Jasmine, do you remember, Roman?" She stepped into the suite and Roman followed her inside.

Now, I considered myself a proficient enough dodger and liar. I'd had to keep my life as a stripper a secret and lie to Kenny and everyone else for years. But in the past, I'd always had time to figure out what to do, what to say.

Roman saved me though. He spoke before I started babbling. "I guess you don't remember me. From the other night," he said, as if he hadn't made love to me a dozen times in the last twelve hours. "I was one of the dancers at your bachelorette party."

"Oh, yeah," I said, hardly able to breathe. What was this guy up to? I began to wonder what I'd thought before: was this dude some kind of crazy?

"I bumped into Roman as I was walking to the elevator," Kyla said. "He offered to help me bring all this stuff up."

"You should've had a bellman do that," I said to Kyla, taking the garment bag and suitcase from Roman's grasp. My hands shook, but it was good that I had something to do so neither one of them would notice.

Roman said, "Oh, I didn't mind helping. I was just leaving the hotel."

With my back to Roman and Kyla, I closed my eyes and took a deep breath. "Well, thank you," I said, when I finally had the nerve to face him.

"Yes, thanks," Kyla added.

The three of us stood there for the longest moments of my life. Roman looked like he was waiting for an invitation to stay.

He *was* some kind of crazy! I needed to get this guy out of here. "Well," I said, hoping that was a good enough hint.

"Well," Kyla said, looking at Roman too.

He still stood there, silent. Until, "Oh, yeah. You're getting married today. You probably need some time to get ready." He stepped back, and I almost tripped rushing past him to get to the door first. It took everything inside of me not to reach out, grab his hand, drag him away, and then push him out the door. But I didn't have to touch him, thank God; he followed me, and when he got to the door, he paused and grinned. "I hope you have a good wedding."

I glared back at him. "Thank you," I said stiffly.

It still took him a moment before he stepped into the hall. I didn't know if he turned back or not because the moment he cleared the door, I shut it behind him.

"That was weird, huh?" Kyla said.

My best friend had absolutely no idea.

She continued, "When I saw him downstairs, he said he was visiting his girlfriend."

"Really?"

"Yeah. It wasn't like I asked him anything. He just kept talking and I kept listening."

"What else did he say?" I really wanted to change the subject, but I felt like I needed to know everything.

It wasn't that I was curious; I needed to figure out just how crazy this dude was.

"He just talked about his girlfriend. Told me that she was the love of his life and how she had been engaged to someone else when they met."

"What?" was what I thought. "Wow," was what I said.

"I know!" Kyla said. "Then he started asking me questions. He wanted to know what I was doing here, and after he had shared all of that, I felt like I had to tell him."

She chuckled, but I didn't.

"I told him that you were getting married today," she continued, "but he didn't really remember you...which was weird. 'Cause he remembered me and he spent all of that time talking to you!" Kyla shrugged. "Well anyway, enough about that guy. This is your day. And it's all about you." She scurried over and hugged me. "Did I come too early? Did I wake you?"

"Nah," I said with my voice so shaky. My heart still hadn't returned to its normal beat, but I wasn't worried about Kyla noticing. She would just chalk it up to pre-wedding nerves. "I've been up for a while."

"Couldn't sleep, huh?" Kyla laughed. Thank God she didn't wait for me to answer. She said, "It was just like that for me too, remember? I tossed and turned the whole night before my wedding. I bet you did that too."

Yup, I had done some tossing and turning last night. But now it was my stomach that was flipping and flopping.

Turning away from me, she said, "This place is beautiful!" Her voice was filled with wonder as she strolled through the living room.

For the first time since I'd opened the door for Kyla, my thoughts turned to something that could make me smile. Kyla's reaction was exactly what I wanted. Everything in her life was always exceptional and next to her, I'd always felt so average. But today, she would be in awe of me.

"I would've loved to have stayed here with you last night," she said as she stood at the balcony window. She pressed her face against the glass, and I cringed a little. If she'd known what had gone down right where she stood, just a couple of hours ago, she would have backed up for real. And now that my thoughts were back to Roman, my smile faded.

"Well anyway, I'm here now." She turned back to me. And then, as if she was looking at me for the first time, she gasped, "Your hair!"

"I know!" I was so glad to have something else to focus on. "But you can hook me up, right?"

She sighed like it was going to be a big task, but her grin told me that she was up for it. "Well, we'd better get started. We only have," she glanced at her watch, "five hours before you become a wife like me!" She squealed, jumped up and down and clapped her hands, reminding me of our days together in kindergarten.

"I'd better get in the shower, I guess. Serena should be here in a little while, and then the wedding planner said she wanted to go over some things with me."

"Okay. Do you want me to order up something for you to eat?"

I paused. When was the last time I ate? Dang – I'd spent all those hours having sex. Food didn't matter.

And now, I didn't want a thing. Roman had stolen my appetite.

"I'm not hungry."

"I'm gonna order you something anyway," she said as she shooed me away. "Now get going. I'll take care of everything."

She laughed and I tried to laugh, too. But it was hard because I didn't feel the joy that I was supposed to on my wedding day. My head was filled with thoughts of Roman. Was that guy weird or what? Was it just a coincidence that he'd bumped into Kyla? That didn't seem likely, because he had left with enough time to be far away from the hotel by the time she'd driven up.

I took a deep breath. Well, at least he was gone and any thoughts I'd had of going down to the beach just to say hello were totally gone, too! I was going to stay as far away from crazy as I could.

Inside the bathroom, I turned the hot water knob all the way to the right, then stood under the shower, taking as much heat as I could stand. I scrubbed away my sins, removed every memory of Roman, and prepared myself for my husband. Kenny was the only one on my mind. Maybe last night with Roman was a good thing; now, I really couldn't wait to get married.

Chapter 6

"Okay, go!" Yolanda, the wedding planner barked at Kyla. She waited for a count of three and said, "Next," then pushed my sister through the double French doors before she closed them and motioned for me and my father to step from the side. "This is what happens when you don't have a rehearsal," Yolanda mumbled under her breath.

She had been complaining so much the whole morning that I'd already learned how to tune her out.

"You ready to do this, sweetheart?" my father asked me as if he was ignoring Yolanda, too.

"Definitely."

He took my hand and hooked our arms together. "Kenny is a good man, but with you by his side, he's a blessed man."

I smiled at him. Even though my dad never lived up to the standards that I'd wanted (he never wore a suit to work like Kyla's father, and he never made a lot of money like Kyla's father) he gave me something better than all of that: he gave me unconditional love.

"I love you, Daddy," I said, right before I kissed his cheek.

"I love you too, sweetheart. And I know your mother is smiling down on you right now."

Ah, man! I was doing just fine up to this moment. My dad bringing up my mother brought new tears to my eyes. I tried to blink them back, because if I started crying again, I might never stop. And Kyla would kill me after all she'd done on my makeup. But how could I help it? Thoughts of my mother always made me want to cry. No matter how much I loved my father, there was nothing like my mother's love. From as early as I could remember, we'd always been a twosome. Even after Serena was born, nothing changed; I was always her special little girl.

You've been with me the longest, was something that she always said to me. You will always have a special place in my heart.

My mother proved to me that she meant it, too. From the manis and pedis that we got together to our monthly pajama parties where my mom slept in my bedroom with me, I knew there was a place that was all mine in her heart.

I know a lot of people thought that I'd changed when my mom passed away. I had to agree. When they lowered my mother into the ground, I was absolutely sure that a piece of my heart went down there with her.

Just as I felt myself dipping down into that abyss of sadness, I was shocked out of it by the wedding planner from hell.

"Okay, get ready, get ready," Yolanda barked. "Time to go. One, two, three..."

She opened the door. My father and I stood under the arch at the entrance of the room. I grasped my father's arm a bit tighter as the world-renowned harpist, Latricia Flowers, softly played her rendition of Stevie Wonder's "You and I."

All of the fifty guests that Kenny and I had invited stood as I took my first steps. Their smiles greeted me, and I took the time to soak in the good wishes that I saw on my friends' faces. Well, calling these people friends might have been a stretch, and the expressions on their faces were more scowls than smiles, but since it was my wedding day, I could see whatever I wanted to see on their faces.

Like I said before, women didn't really like me. Not that I cared; I'd stopped caring about what any of them thought the day I graduated from middle school. On that day, I'd left behind every single incident that, if I hadn't been the strong child my parents raised me to be, would've scarred me for life.

On graduation day, I forgot about the time I'd walked into the bathroom and heard the girls talking about the way the heels of my loafers were worn down.

"Do you think Jasmine's ever had a new pair of shoes?" Tiffany Adams had giggled.

I was so crushed that I'd run back into Mrs. Yearwood's math class and when Kyla asked me what was wrong, I shook my head and just prayed my bladder would hold out for the next three hours until I got home.

On graduation day, I pushed aside the hurt I still felt when Brittany Weatherspoon had handed out invitations to her thirteenth birthday party to every student in the class...except for me.

"Oh, Jasmine, I'm sorry," she'd said as I fought hard to hold my tears. "I figured that you wouldn't be able to afford a birthday gift, since you're poor and all, so I was just helping you out."

The only thing that *had* helped me out that day was Kyla standing up and returning her invitation, declaring in front of the whole class that if her best friend wasn't invited then she wasn't going either.

On graduation day, I'd left behind the days of torture, the days of reminders that I wasn't included because I was nothing more than a scholarship student. I'd left behind the tears that I held inside because I would never be one of the girls.

But, on the first day of high school, that had all changed. When Donnell Davis, a sophomore on the varsity basketball team, had winked at me as he strutted by my locker. That single action brought me to the realization that I didn't need girls, I had boys. And the boys turned me into the most popular girl in high school.

If I'd had my way, this little chapel would have been filled with boys who'd grown into men, but there was no way that would've passed by my husband. So women were here, just to fill the chairs.

My eyes scanned the crowd and I focused first on Shelley, standing in the back row like she was only there because she was my boss and as soon as she could, she was gonna make a quick getaway. She wasn't even smiling; she was just staring, and I knew what that was all about – for once, she was jealous of me. I wanted to roll my eyes, but couldn't. Because that would be the precise moment when the photographer, Dee Hampton, would snap a picture. I just prayed that she got some good photos of me, but I wouldn't bet any money on that. I had told Kenny over and over that I didn't want Deborah as our photographer, but he'd insisted on her.

"Come on, you know she needs the work," he'd begged.

It wasn't that I was trying to be cold-hearted. I just didn't think it was proper protocol to have my husband-to-be's ex working our wedding. Okay, so they'd been boyfriend and girlfriend way back in the sixth grade, but it was in the sixth grade where I'd discovered the truth about girls, remember?

Well, whatever! All Deborah could do today was dream about what might have been. I spread my lips into a smile as I took a final look at Shelly, even though all she did was smirk at me. I shook my head just a little, wondering why she was even here. She probably didn't even come with a gift. Not that my boss was cheap. She wore some righteous designer outfits to work just about every day. But she didn't like me, so I doubted if she was going to pull out her Gold American Express card for me.

My smile turned genuine when I saw Laverne and Faith, the two administrative assistants at Carnation. Now those were two ladies that I could say I liked. Laverne was the head assistant and Faith was kinda her sidekick, but from my first day on the job, they took care of me. At first, all I did was wonder: what did they think they were going to get out of me? But it turned out they wanted nothing, and over the years that I'd been there, they always had my back.

As my father and I continued the slow stroll down the aisle, I soaked in the *oohhs* and *aahhs* that softly filled the air, and I knew that I'd achieved the look. I wore a simple dress, but the satin-crepe was cut to my body to hug every curve and the cowl neckline was just low and sexy enough. It was too bad that the designer, LaShawn, wasn't here to see everyone's reaction to her creation. I had invited her, but that chick hadn't even sent back her RSVP. She called me up directly to decline, telling me that she really didn't like me and designing the dress for me had been all about business for her.

Whatever!

My glance moved to the other side and I looked right into the eyes of Alexis Ward and Stephanie Johnson. When I saw the two of them, I didn't even care if the photographer caught me rolling my eyes. What were the two of them doing on the groom's side of the aisle anyway? I bet they did that on purpose. They didn't even know Kenny! Not that they were my friends either. I only knew Alexis and Stephanie because of Kyla, and I wished she'd never introduced me to either one of them. The way they were acting now, I'd bet they wished the same thing. Alexis had the nerve to yawn as I passed by, and Stephanie wasn't even looking; she was studying her nails as if she was trying to figure out if she needed a new manicure.

Whatever!

At least I saw some friendly faces when I looked back to the other side. Well, not friends actually – the second row was filled with my relatives, though I'd only invited a few. I wanted my wedding to be classy, not country, but that was hard to do considering the folks I was related to. Take my cousin, Cheryl. I did love her; she was a sweet kid. But while everyone was standing and looking and appreciating me, Cheryl sat at the end of the row, reading a book! I'm telling you, every time I saw my cousin, she was reading a book. But dang – this was a wedding. Who read a book at a wedding? See, that's why there were only ten of my relatives here, including my dad, my sister, and my brother-in-law.......and then I saw them: my nephews.

Every single bad thought I had up to that moment was all gone because there were Serena's sons, smiling up at me. Serena thought Robert Jr., who was three, and James, who was two, were too young to be in the wedding. But to me they were still part of it, standing there in the front row next to their father, wearing miniature tuxedos. I wanted to rush over, swoop them both into my arms, then pinch and kiss their cheeks. Those little boys had captured my heart the way no one else had, except for....

Kenneth Larson.

When I looked up, Kenny came into my full view and now no one else, not even my nephews, was on my mind. Kenny Larson was decked out for real. I'd gone with Kenny to buy the Pierre Cardin tuxedo that he wore. Of course, he could have rented a tuxedo like every other groom, but I had big plans for him and he was going to need a tuxedo in his wardrobe. And we had picked out the perfect suit. Because looking as dapper as he did, he could leave right now and step into the pages of that hot GQ Magazine.

But it was more than just the way Kenny looked. It was the way he smiled, no, the way he beamed as his eyes stayed on me. I swear, that man didn't even blink as my father guided me closer to him.

In Kenny's eyes I saw it – just pure love. Like he loved me more than anything in the world. Like he would always love me that way.

And I loved him so much too.

I had no doubts and now I could leave what I'd done last night and all those nights before in the same place – I could leave my dirty laundry in the past. What was before me now was a future that I'd dreamed about since I was a little girl. Kenny was my prince. No, he wasn't going to be the NFL star that I always thought he'd be, but he was still mine. And together, we'd build a great life and have it all: a new house, wonderful children, successful careers. Nothing and no one else would matter as long as it was just the two of us.

By the time I reached Kenny and the judge, my eyes were filled with tears, but my heart was singing.

My father stood on one side and Kenny stood on the other as we faced the judge. I'd met the judge last week, at the wedding planner's suggestion. Yolanda told me that there were still many people who didn't believe in being married by a woman. It didn't matter to me — as long as the person spoke a language that I could understand and would help me say, 'I do,' I didn't care a bit about gender. But I was glad that I'd met Judge Juanita Davis. When we'd met at the hotel's bar, she was nothing like I'd expected a black-robe-wearing judge to be. She wasn't stiff; she wasn't staid. She was so cool, dressed in a rhinestone-studded jean pants suit and tossing back tequila shots like they were nothing more than the red Kool-Aid that Kenny loved so much. Being with her was like hanging out with a girlfriend. Not that we would ever be friends. She'd given me her number, but I'd thrown it into the trash can before I even left the hotel. Like I said, I didn't trust women, not even if they wore black robes.

My father, Kenny, and I stood in front of the judge and waited for Latricia to finish the last stanza of the song. At the end, the guests applauded politely. Latricia smiled and glanced over at Kenny, but when she looked at me, she rolled her eyes.

Dang! I hope no one saw that. She was just mad because when she'd met with me and Yolanda, she had thirty different songs that she wanted to play – and I didn't like a single one of them. But Latricia needed to understand that this was my wedding and she was being paid to do what I told her to do. So she could make all the faces she wanted. I was the queen today.

Once the applause was over, Judge Davis smiled at me and Kenny before she said, "Dearly beloved...."

The wonderful thing about having a judge and not a traditional pastor was that we wouldn't have to go through all that mumbo-jumbo that came with preachers. Juanita had told me that her job was to marry us – get us in and get us out. Then we could get to the four-hour reception, which was the main part of the party to me.

Standing next to Kenny, though, I didn't want to think about any of that. Instead, I wanted to think about the first time I'd laid eyes on this man, though calling him a man was a stretch back then. We were just high school kids who thought we were grown. But though I'd had the attention of plenty of boys, Kenny was the only one who touched my heart, who made me understand love from someone besides my mother and father.

"Who gives this woman to be married to this man?"

"I do," my father said. My father kissed my cheek, shook Kenny's hand, then sat on the front pew.

I'd told Judge Davis to keep out that line about if anyone objected to this marriage. Not that I thought any of the men from my past would show up; I was worried about what some crazed woman might do. Some jealous woman jumping up and telling a lie. So many lies had been told about me that I wasn't about to take a chance.

So the judge just kept reading from her little black book, and I just kept hoping that this would be over quick. Facing Kenny, we exchanged vows, made eternal promises to love each other forever, for always, and then stood holding hands as L. Alexander, a local up-and-coming R&B singer, sang *Born Again*. L. stood just a few feet from the judge – and she was wearing white!

What?

She was singing at my wedding and she was wearing white? Wasn't she aware of the fact that the bride was always the star?

With a sigh, I turned away and a smile was back on my face as I looked into Kenny's eyes the entire time L. sang. He squeezed my hands and I knew what he was thinking. And for the first time in a long time, I was right there with him. I couldn't wait to be alone with my husband. I couldn't wait to show him just how much I loved him.

At the end of the song, our guests stood up, giving L. a standing ovation. Now, I admit, she did sing that song, but it felt like she was trying to steal my show. First her white dress and then that performance.

She was supposed to sing again at the luncheon, but I started thinking that maybe I should send L. home. My cousin, Trina, could fill in for her. Not that Trina could carry a note, but she didn't seem to know that. With Trina singing, all of the attention would definitely stay on me.

"Well, all right now," Judge Davis said.

She added a few closing words, and just like she promised, she had us in and out.

"Jasmine Cox and Kenneth Larson, I now pronounce that you are one and you are man and wife." As the guests clapped, the judge continued, "Kenny, you may kiss the bride."

Everyone cheered as Kenny held me in his arms and tried to thrust his tongue all the way down my throat. If he could have, I was sure that he probably would have ripped my dress off of me right there. I laughed when he allowed me to come up for air.

I was so happy. So ready to be his wife.

"Ladies and gentlemen, I present to you for the first time, Mr. and Mrs. Kenneth Larson."

I held my husband's hand as we walked back down the aisle, past all the faces that I saw before. This time, though everyone was smiling...Alexis, Stephanie, and even my boss, Shelly.

But as I looked at my boss, my steps slowed down. Because next to Shelly, in that last row, standing right next to her, was Roman.

Now, I can't say that I had too much of God in my life, but He had to be right there with me at that moment because that was the only way I was able to keep walking. What I really wanted to do was fall out right there.

What was he doing here? Did he know Shelly? If he knew my boss, that would be a disaster!

It was difficult, but I kept putting one foot in front of the other, holding onto Kenny even tighter than I held him before. But my eyes stayed on Roman. He blended in with the rest of the guests, especially since he wore a tailored blue suit. But I couldn't even appreciate how good he looked 'cause my heart was filled with fear. In the next second, though, he was out of my line of vision as Kenny and I stepped into the hallway.

"Come here, come here," Yolanda clapped her hands. She was trying to set us up in the reception line so that we could greet our guests and send them into the banquet room for the lunch reception.

But there was no way we could do this line out here. I had to get to Roman – find out what he was up to and then do everything I could to keep him away from Kenny and my father, and my sister. And, oh my God...I had to keep him away from Kyla because she would recognize him after this morning. And Alexis and Stephanie, who were also at the club for my party and saw that man strip down to a G-string. Maybe Alexis and Stephanie wouldn't recognize him with clothes on, but Kyla would.

It was hard to keep my smile and my composure as the wheels in my head churned with everything that could go wrong.

"Baby," I whispered to Kenny, "I want to run into the restroom before we greet everyone."

"Oh, okay. No problem. I can hold it down until you come back."

"No, you know what?" I said. "Why don't we just move the reception line into the room where we're having lunch? I never really understood why they wanted us in the hall anyway."

Kenny frowned. "Can we just change it like that? What is Yolanda going to say?"

Inside my head, I screamed. Who cared what that barracuda thought? But on the outside, all I did was kiss his lips lightly. "Isn't this our day? We should be able to do whatever we want."

As the rest of the bridal party rushed up behind us to offer their congratulations, Kenny called Yolanda over to tell her the change of plans. I saw her sigh, but

I didn't have time to focus on her. My eyes were on the guests who were strolling out of the room. My eyes searched the hall for a place where I could talk to Roman, away from the prying eyes of my friends and family.

"What's wrong?" Kyla asked me.

"Oh, nothing. I just...have to go to the bathroom."

That was supposed to be good enough. That was supposed to get me some time alone to handle Roman. But I forgot there was a reason why they were called my bridesmaids.

"Not without us," Kyla said as if she and my sister were my bodyguards. Behind her, Serena nodded.

"No, really, I'm fine," I said. "Truly, I can do this by myself. Trust me. I've gone to the bathroom before."

Serena and Kyla laughed.

"But you haven't gone as a wife." The two gave each other high-five as if they belonged to some special wives' club and I was a new member.

"We're coming with you," Serena said, "so just shut up and lead the way so that we can get back to the celebration."

I tried to laugh and act like all was well. It was hard now because the hall was filling up with our guests. My eyes scanned the space, but though I saw everyone who'd been inside the room, I didn't see Roman. I shook my head slightly. Could I have imagined him?

But the moment I had that thought, I spotted him. At the other end of the hall, by the elevators that led to the lobby – that led to the entrance, or the exit in this case. He was close enough for me to see him, but far enough away that nobody would really notice me looking at him.

So no one else saw the way he smiled. And no one else saw the way he blew me a kiss before he disappeared into the elevators.

I closed my eyes and exhaled a long breath of relief. At least he was gone. But as I followed my sister and Kyla into the restroom, I didn't really feel any better. That was so bizarre. What was that man doing here? And the real question: was he coming back?

I tried to smile and primp and joke with my sister and best friend as we stood in front of the bathroom mirror, but it was hard to focus.

All I could think about was: what kind of madness had I gotten myself into?

Chapter 7

Kenny Larson and I were going to be married forever – because there was no way that I could go through another afternoon like this. Not that the reception was all that bad. If I ignored the fact that there were tables filled with women who couldn't even find it in their hearts to give me my props – not even on my big day – it would've been quite a celebration. Especially having my new husband by my side. Kenny held onto my hand as if we were one for real and I have to admit that I loved it. I didn't expect to feel this way. In the past, if Kenny had stayed too close to me, I would've told him to stop being so clingy.

But today, it was like something happened from the moment I said, 'I do.' Today, I didn't care if he was clinging to me because I didn't want to let go of him myself. Maybe it was because I finally realized that I really was totally and completely in love with this man.

Or maybe it was because of Roman.

I held my breath for four hours, wondering when he was going to return. Not that I wanted him to come back. God, no! But the thing was, I didn't know if he would. I was still trying to figure out why he'd shown up at my wedding in the first place. The image of him standing there next to my boss, Shelly, haunted me through the entire reception. Had he somehow shown up with Shelly? Like, was he her date? That would've been a disaster, since Shelly and I shared mutual feelings of strong dislike for each other.

As Kenny and I moved from table to table greeting our guests – and accepting the envelopes that I prayed were filled with lots of money – I kept one eye on the door. And as Kenny and I shared our first "married" meal together, I watched for signs of Roman. Even when we swayed together for our first dance, I positioned Kenny so that when I looked over his shoulder, I could see the door in case I had to make a run for it. But as Kenny and I danced, the only thing I saw was my boss sneaking out after she'd eaten all of my food.

There was no sign of Roman, and for the last hour of the party, I breathed and enjoyed myself, at least with my family. Especially my nephews. Those little boys loved to dance. As I carried James in my arms and held onto Junior's hand, we danced to every Michael Jackson song that the DJ played.

Finally, the reception was over. And to tell you the truth, I was shocked that Roman hadn't appeared again. He hadn't shown up and destroyed my five-hour marriage.

"Okay," Yolanda, the planner-from-hell, yelled. "Let's line up." She clapped her hands and screeched some more.

Yolanda gathered the guests and directed them to stand on either side of the door, creating a center aisle for me and Kenny.

"What is this?" I asked Yolanda. This hadn't been part of the plan.

Her lips spread into a sinister smile. "This is a surprise. Something special I put together just for you." She motioned for me and Kenny to walk down that lane.

When that first grain of rice slapped me on my cheek, I was pissed. Kenny laughed and ducked down as grown men and women tossed rice at us. The guests cheered and I winced. Those morsels felt like lethal weapons every time I got popped on my bare arms or someone hit me with a shot in my face.

I knew a couple of those women were taking direct aim at me. Especially Alexis and Stephanie. The two stood shoulder-to-shoulder with sadistic smiles on their faces and rice piled high in their hands.

But I weathered it all like the champ that I was and as Kenny held my hand, I dragged him as quickly as I could down that torture lane.

"Have a good honeymoon!"

"Wishing you God's blessings."

"Don't do anything I wouldn't do!"

That last bit of advice came from the wedding planner!

I was more than relieved when Kenny and I stepped out into the hallway, but before I rushed away from everyone, I wanted to say goodbye to the people who mattered to me.

"I'm so happy for you," Kyla said as she hugged me. "Kenny is a good man. Always remember that."

She didn't have to worry. I knew that now and I would remember it always. Kenny Larson was a do-right man, better than the hundreds of men I'd met in the club all combined and definitely better than that psycho Roman who, thank God, I would never see again.

I kissed my father, hugged my sister, and wrapped my nephews in my arms.

"Where you going, Auntie?" Junior asked me.

"I'm going on my honeymoon."

"Can we go with you?" James asked.

I laughed. "No, not this time, but you know what?"

"What?" my nephews said together.

"I'll bring you both back something fabulous!"

"Yay!" James cheered.

"From where?" Junior asked.

"From my honeymoon," I said. I was still excited about the fact that I was going to some unknown exotic location. Just the thought of that made me want Kenny even more.

I gave my nephew's a final kiss, then took hold of my husband's hand and smiled. He gazed into my eyes like I was the most beautiful woman he'd ever seen, and I was sure that I was.

Now, I was ready to begin our new, wonderful life together.

Kenny didn't even let the door to the bridal suite close before his lips were all over me. He smothered me with soft kisses, gentle kisses. And I was caught up in his rapture as he carried me from the hotel's threshold into the bedroom.

It wasn't until he laid me on the bed that my eyes popped open and I pushed him off of me.

"What happened?" he asked, his face crinkled with confusion.

"Nothing, nothing," I said, as I closed my eyes tightly and tried to push back the images. Dang! How was I supposed to lay down with my husband on the same bed where Roman tried to break my back last night? I hadn't thought this part all the way through because if I had, I would've never let Roman ravish my body in what was supposed to be my bridal bed.

"Jasmine," Kenny called me away from my thoughts. "What's wrong?"

I had to come up with something quick. "Really, it's nothing. I...I was just thinking that...this is gonna be our first time as man and wife. I want to take it slow. I want it to be special."

His smile was so full of love that I wanted to take back that lie.

"From the moment you said, 'I do,' this has been special for me. And this," he pressed his lips against my neck, "and this," now he went for my nose, "and this!" He ended his words with a kiss and I returned his emotion.

I pushed back every thought, each image I had of me and Roman together in this bed, and it was easy at first because all I wanted to do was love my husband. But as soon as I hit the sheets, it was Roman's lips on mine and Roman's hands on me.

I couldn't take it.

This time, when I sat straight up, I pulled Kenny up with me.

"What the....?"

He didn't get the chance to finish – my lips were all over his. I led him into the bathroom and while we were still connected, I tore the tuxedo from his body as he ripped the dress from mine.

"Why the bathroom?" he asked when our lips parted for just an instant.

"Because we've never done this before. I want us to take our first shower together."

He grinned. "Kinky!"

Kinky? Not so much! If Kenny only knew the number of men who'd had me in a shower....but it didn't matter. *He and I* had never done this before, and for me, this was the only time that it would count.

Kenny turned on the water in the over-sized stall to full blast, checked the temperature and then asked, "What about your hair?"

I answered him by pushing him into the shower until he was against the marble wall, and with the shower's rain pelting gently against my back, I knelt before my husband.

He closed his eyes and groaned and moaned and shuddered as if he was a teenager and this was his first time. But he couldn't help it. Kenny didn't know that he was in the *hands* of an expert. With the skills that came from my years of practice, I showed him how happy I was to be his wife.

We made love in the shower for what felt like hours, until our skin was too pickled to stay there any longer. But Kenny wasn't finished and when he carried me from the bathroom to the bedroom and gently laid me down atop the satin duvet, this time, I was able to enjoy every inch of my husband, every moment of our consummation. Now, I had no thoughts of any other man, no memories of what had gone on in this bed just twenty-four hours before. My thoughts were only of Kenny Larson.

Roman had been washed away in the shower and I was clean...as clean as any virginal bride.

Chapter 8

Lifting my head up just a bit so that I could glance at the clock on the table next to the bed, I was shocked to see that it was already after ten. Had we slept this late?

I couldn't believe it, but I shouldn't have been surprised. What else could either of us do after making non-stop marital love? I grinned – all the men I'd been with, and the most memorable now was last night with Kenny.

Rolling over, I propped myself up on my elbow and stared at the man who was making it so easy for me to love him again. His lips were parted, just slightly; he slept silently.

My husband!

It was hard for me to believe that it had finally happened. I'd wanted Kenny for so long, had wished for it so much, and now I was lying next to him with a ring on my finger. He looked peaceful. And happy. He slept with a smile that I was glad I'd put on his face.

I could've watched him for the rest of the day, but I knew that we had to get going. Kenny hadn't told me anything about our honeymoon plans – not the time we were leaving nor our destination. But I was sure that we couldn't stay in bed much longer. We had to be leaving for the airport soon.

Last night had been exciting and romantic enough, but now it was time to take this honeymoon up a notch. He had been so secretive; I couldn't imagine where he was taking me. Were we going to be making sweet love on some Caribbean beach? Or kissing under the stars in Hawaii? Or professing our love to each other on the top of the Eiffel Tower?

That last thought may have been a bit of a stretch - there was no way Kenny could afford a trip to Europe. But that was okay...wherever we ended up, we'd be together and I'd get to love my husband all day and all night long in some tropical paradise. I knew this upcoming week was going to be one I would always remember.

Giving my husband a gentle shove, I called his name, "Kenny."

He didn't move.

"Baby. Come on. We have to get up."

With his eyes still closed, he stretched a bit in his sleep. Then his eyes opened slowly and his smile widened into a grin.

"Good morning, wife," he said through a throat that was still filled with sleep.

Now I was the one grinning. "Good morning, husband." I wasn't big on any contact with my partner before he or I took care of our morning breath issues, but this was one time when it didn't matter. Maybe it was that husband thing, I don't know. But Kenny didn't taste half-bad.

After at least a dozen kisses, I pulled back. "Baby, we have to get up and get going." Pushing myself from the bed, I stood, excited, ready to get to the real honeymoon. "So, where are we going and what time do we have to get to the airport?"

It wasn't until Kenny's eyes roamed over me that I remembered that I was standing there naked. Inside, I sighed. Really? Did a naked body break all men's concentration so easily? Dang! Women could solve all the world's problems with these kinds of abilities. Just send a delegation of shapely, butt-naked women to negotiate with the heads of state of any foreign country, and the U.S. would have nothing but peace and power.

I laughed.

"What's so funny?" Kenny was still stretched out in the bed, only now his head was propped up as he rested on his elbow.

"Nothing," I said. I reached for his arm and tried to pull him up. "Come on. We have to get going. What time is our flight?"

But instead of me pulling him up, Kenny snatched me down and I flopped onto the bed.

"I have a surprise for you," he said.

"What?"

He pulled me into his arms and grinned like he had big news.

Oh, my goodness...were we going to Europe? My heart started beating so fast.

He said, "We're going to begin our life as husband and wife in totally luxury."

We *were* going to Europe! Already I was imagining the beaches of Cannes and Nice. Weren't they topless? Oh, if this man was taking me to Europe, I was going to give it to him good! It would take him weeks to recover from the things I planned to do to him on our honeymoon.

He said, "We're going to stay here – in the Ritz Carlton – in this suite. And with room service and this grand bed, we never have to get up and go anywhere!"

It took a moment for my brain to understand what my ears had heard. I pushed myself away from Kenny and stood up and with my hands on my hips.

"Repeat that, please?" because I wanted to give him a chance to take back that lie that he'd just told.

He grinned even wider. "We're gonna stay here, baby. I know how much you love the Ritz." He sat up. "And all of this," he spread his arms wide as if he was giving me the world, "all of this is yours for a week. I arranged it with the hotel last month. Isn't this great?"

I didn't even wait a beat. "You have got to be kidding me."

It was my tone and my stance that probably gave Kenny the first clue that I was not impressed. "Are you serious!" I tried not to shout. "You want me to spend my honeymoon here? In Los Angeles?"

"Not in L.A., baby. Here in the Ritz Carlton. I thought you loved this hotel."

"I do. And for my honeymoon, I expected to be in a Ritz somewhere in another country."

He rolled over to the edge of the bed, propped himself up onto his knees and reached for me. But I stepped back, far from his embrace.

"Baby, what's wrong?"

"Are you really asking me that?" I crossed my arms. "Kenny, please tell me that you're kidding."

He frowned. "I thought you would love this idea. It's not like we'll ever leave the hotel – no matter where we go. So I thought, why not stay here and save the travel time?"

"No, you thought, why not stay here and save the travel money." My anger was building and I stomped my foot. "Kenny, I told you that I would pay for the honeymoon, but you insisted."

"Whether you paid or I paid, it wouldn't have made any difference. I thought...I think this is a great idea. You said yourself that this is a beautiful suite."

"Yeah, for me to spend the night *before* my wedding and the night *of* my wedding, but I don't want to spend my honeymoon here."

He shook his head. "I'm sorry. I thought you'd love this idea as much as I did."

I glared at him and he held his arms out to me. "Jasmine, babe, come here. I promise you, we're gonna have a good time." Once again, his glance took in every inch of my nakedness, and I grabbed the coverlet that was tossed over the lounger for decoration, covering as much of my body as I could. Kenny didn't deserve to see me naked.

"Jasmine," he began as I wrapped myself up, "come on. This is going to be wonderful...I promise."

I didn't say a word to him. I just stomped out of the room.

"Jasmine!"

I slammed the bathroom door and then stood with my back against it. I could not believe this was happening to me. I was born in L.A., raised in L.A., had gone to college in L.A., and now I was going to spend my honeymoon...in L.A.?

I wasn't the kind of girl who cried; I had been through too much for that. But something came over me now. I wasn't sure if it was the expectation or the disappointment that filled my eyes with tears.

Turning back to the door, I clicked the lock, then dragged myself to the vanity. In the mirror, I stared at my reflection – tearful eyes and a face stretched with sorrow. Definitely, there were many occasions in my life that were more painful than this. But in this moment, at this time, all I could think about was the hurt that I felt right now. Why hadn't Kenny taken the time to plan our honeymoon as he promised? Did he not think I was worth it?

Or maybe it wasn't him at all. Maybe it was all me. Had I just made the biggest mistake of my life? Was I going to be able to live with a man as ordinary as Kenny?

Those questions made me weak, made me crumble to the floor. And now I cried, for real.

Hours passed before I unlocked the door and came out of the bathroom, now wrapped in one of the thick, oversized towels. Kenny sat on the edge of the bed, covered by nothing, but his face drooped with the same sadness I felt. I couldn't figure out why *he* was sad.

"Jasmine, I'm sorry," he whispered.

I didn't bother to look at him as I searched the bedroom for my overnight bag. Was I going to have to put on the same clothes that I'd worn to the hotel?

This was un-freaking-believable.

As if he read my mind, Kenny said, "I brought a suitcase from home for you. It's in the closet."

I could have said thank you, but I didn't even have that many words inside of me for him. I stomped to the closet, rolled out the suitcase, hoisted it onto the lounger, and unzipped the bag.

My first thought when I looked inside was, "This fool done brought me somebody else's clothes." Kenny sidled up behind me and I cringed as he pressed his desire for me against my behind and wrapped his arms around my waist.

"Baby, I'm sorry, but I was thinking about better ways to spend our money. So one of the things I did was go out and buy you a couple of new outfits." He chuckled a bit, though he didn't sound too happy. "Actually, I didn't pick out a thing, so you don't have to worry about that. This suitcase is filled with all new clothes that Kyla, Alexis, and Stephanie picked out for you."

My first thought was there was not one of the three who I would've taken shopping with me. Yes, Kyla was my best friend, and we would be cool forever, but the girl dressed like a boring doctor's wife. And Alexis and Stephanie? Please. I wouldn't ask them to buy me a bag of rocks.

Kenny whispered in my ear. "Really, baby. I put a lot of thought into all of this. I was trying to make you happy with surprises for you all through the week. This is the first one."

Okay, so at least he had thought about something. First I pulled out a gorgeous purple oversized top with major Dynasty-style shoulder pads and an acid-washed denim mini-skirt. I loved it. With each new top, and pair of jeans, and Members Only jackets I pulled out of the suitcase, another tear was wiped away. I couldn't believe Kyla and her buddies had done right by me.

He said, "Do you see anything you like?"

Was he kidding me? I loved every single thing in this suitcase, but I wasn't about to admit that because fabulous clothes did not make up for the fact that I'd still be spending my honeymoon in L.A.

"There are a few things that are okay," I said, trying hard to be nonchalant. I mean, don't get me wrong: I'd been given much nicer, much more expensive things by any number of my *dates*. But this all did feel really special coming from Kenny. I just didn't want him to know that yet.

"I have a suggestion." His arms were still wrapped around me, his lips were still close to my ear. I prayed that he wasn't going to say anything about making love right now because he wasn't getting any. He could believe that!

He said, "Although all I wanted to do was spend the next seven days in bed with my wife, let's go out for a while, hang out, maybe get something to eat."

I didn't think it was possible, but his words took me into further depression. What were we going to do? Where were we going to eat? Maybe he planned to take me to Yee's, the around-the-way Chinese restaurant where we (and everyone else) always got our take-out. Or were we going to venture to M&M's, which is where we ate when we were in a soul-food state of mind.

This was ridiculous.

But maybe going out was the best thing. It wasn't like I really wanted to stay in this room and sit and stare into the face of the new husband who had disappointed me. I grabbed the purple top and mini-skirt. With a scowl on my face, I looked the outfit over, as if I wasn't pleased. This was gonna look so cute on me.

Without a word to Kenny, I tossed the two pieces over my arm, grabbed a pair of panties and marched right back into the bathroom because like I said before, Kenny didn't deserve to see me naked.

I heard his deep sigh right before I slammed the bathroom door and locked it behind me.

I was bored. No. "Bored" was too nice a word, too soft for what I was feeling. The word for my emotion hadn't been invented yet. They also hadn't invented the word for what I wanted to do to my new husband, because "killing," "murder" – again, too soft, too nice.

We had spent the afternoon riding through Los Angeles as if we were tourists. The only thing missing were those big ole cameras hanging from our necks as Kenny dragged me from the LaBrea Tar Pits and then onto the Hollywood Walk of Fame. My husband did this with the excitement of a first time visitor to the city, rather than the natives we both were.

With each new destination, my disgust grew.

"Come on, Jasmine. We never had a chance to do any of these things before."

"There was a reason for that."

"My thought was that we could do this together, have fun without any other relatives around, see all of these sights without the pressure of having to be somewhere else in an hour."

"Whooohooo!"

The look on Kenny's face was one of pure pain as if his feelings were so deeply hurt. But there was nothing I could do about that, no way I could help him because while his feelings were hurt, my heart was broken.

As the minutes moved into hours, my depression deepened.

Which was why I was sitting now in our car with my head back and my eyes closed. I figured as long as my eyes stayed shut, my mouth would too. And me staying silent was a major benefit to my husband – he just didn't know that.

I felt the car come to a stop, but I didn't even bother to open my eyes. Based on what we'd already been through, I figured why waste my time trying to see nothing?

Kenny said, "I thought we'd get something to eat down here."

With a sigh, I slowly opened my eyes and my heart started thumping. No, again, I was using the wrong word. Because, thumping was clearly too soft for a heart that was trying to escape from one's chest.

"What are we doing here?" I asked, taking in the horizon over the Pacific Ocean.

"I wanted to go someplace we've never gone before."

"Venice Beach? We've been here a million times."

"But we've never been to that restaurant, the one of the edge of the boardwalk where we can just sit and people watch."

"Oh...kay," was all I said, though I wanted to grumble some more. I wanted to fuss and pick a fight so that Kenny would want to leave this place and take me back to the Ritz.

"Come on, Jasmine. I'm trying to do something right here. How many times have we passed that place, but it was always so crowded? I thought you would've love to have lunch on the beach."

"I'll just sit in the car."

Kenny looked at me as if I'd lost my mind. "You're that mad at me? That you'd rather not eat."

"It's not that."

"Then what is it?"

I'd already been to that restaurant – with the man I slept with the night before our wedding.

But of course I didn't say that aloud. So when he looked at me with eyes full of sorrow, I released a big sigh so that he would know how much of a chore this was for me. I opened the door, slid out of the car and as Kenny came around to the passenger side, I tried to imagine all the scenarios that could possibly happen and come up with a ready solution for each one.

When Kenny reached for my hand, I held onto him this time. Not because my attitude had changed, but because I needed to hold him to maneuver us through the masses more easily – and to pull him quickly past the cage of Muscle Beach.

My greatest hope was that Roman wasn't at the beach at all. I mean, today was Sunday; most likely he had the day off. And even if he was working, the boardwalk was thick with the typical Sunday-in-August crowd. With any luck, he wouldn't see us if he was here.

With each step we took, I kept my eyes straight ahead, my focus on our destination...or at least *my* destination, which was to get through this and get past Roman. On our left were the paddle tennis courts with, as always, bikini and Speedo-clad players. To the right were the T-shirt shops and tattoo parlors.

Our pace was slow enough for Kenny not to feel like we were in some kind of race, but brisk enough for me to feel like I was making progress. Not that getting by the cage was going to be good enough; it was clear that Roman frequented that beach-side restaurant often, so he could show up there too. But I kept my focus on what could happen first. I'd worry about the restaurant once we got there.

As we edged closer to Muscle Beach, I kept my head down and stayed to the right. Covered by the crowd, I felt like a Bond girl trying to escape from a gang of international killers.

And then through the summer sounds of Venice Beach – the chatter of the pedestrians, the music from the boom boxes, the cries of victory from the paddle tennis players – I heard, "Jasmine!"

I tucked my chin down into my chest even further and picked up the pace as if I heard nothing.

"Jasmine!"

My prayer was that all that Kenny heard was the chatter, and the music, and the competitive shouts. But then he added his own call.

"Jasmine," Kenny said, "I think someone is calling you."

I stopped and did a half-turn, not daring to look behind me. "I didn't hear anything." I tried to keep it moving, but then the shout came again.

"Jasmine!"

This time, Kenny stopped completely. "Okay, you can't tell me that you didn't hear that." He looked behind us. "Yeah, it's that guy. The one waving his arms. He's calling you."

It was only because I didn't have any choice that my glance followed where my husband pointed. And two seconds later, my indiscretion was standing right in front of me.

"Hey," Roman said. Sweat poured off his bald head, though he wasn't out of breath. "I thought that was you."

"Hey," was all I said, hoping that would be enough for him and that he'd have the good sense to turn around and leave me alone.

"So," Roman looked from me to Kenny and then back again, "what's up?"

I couldn't believe this. I couldn't believe that Roman would run up on me like this, like we were friends. And now, he wanted to stay and chat like we were *old* friends. Was he kidding me? Was this cat that crazy?

Kenny looked from me to Roman, back to me, then to Roman before he frowned and held out his hand. "Hey, bro. I'm Kenny, Jasmine's husband."

"Oh, yeah. Yeah. Right. Nice to meet you, man." Turning to me, he said, "I heard you got married."

Kenny answered for me. "Yes, we did. Just yesterday, in fact."

"Well, congratulations," Roman said.

Kenny thanked him, but I just stood there, numb and dumb.

"So, what are you guys up to? Not going on a honeymoon?"

"Oh yeah, you know it, bro." And the two men laughed like they were really brothers. Kenny wrapped his arms all around me. "We just decided to hang here in L.A. You know, kinda do all the things you never get to do when you're home."

"Oh yeah?"

I couldn't tell if Roman's grin was for me or for Kenny.

Roman said, "That is really cool. Just hanging out at home?"

"Nah, we're in the marina. We got married over there, and it's a beautiful place to spend a week."

Now, I wanted to slap Kenny upside his head. Why was he acting like a girl? Telling all of our business to this nutcase!

But then, Kenny turned the tables. "So," he looked at me, "how do you two know each other?"

I may have been acting dumb, but I couldn't stay mute – especially since I didn't know what crazy Roman would say. So I found my voice right away. "Kyla introduced us," I said. Now, that wasn't totally a lie. If Kyla hadn't dragged me to a bachelorette party that I didn't want to go to, I wouldn't be standing here next to a man I didn't want to be around. It was her fault that I even knew Roman.

"Oh, really?" Kenny said as if he found that hard to believe.

"Yeah," Roman said, joining in my lie. "I've known Kyla for a while now."

"Yeah," Kenny said, looking at Roman a little closer. "You do look familiar. Did we meet at one of their parties or something?"

I was gonna die for sure now. His recognition of Roman had to be from yesterday, when he saw him standing in the back row after we'd exchanged our vows. I prayed that he wouldn't put it together.

"Nah, we've never met; I just got one of those faces." Roman laughed. "If we'd met, I would've remembered you, trust that." He laughed again while Kenny and I just frowned.

"Well, we'd better get going."

Can I tell you how grateful I was that my husband was finally ready to put an end to this little encounter?

"Yeah, okay. You kids have fun on your honeymoon. Nice meeting you, Kenny, and I'll see you around, Jasmine."

Roman looked at me when he said that and my hope was that it was just one of those generic goodbyes. But the way he chuckled as he walked away, I knew that he meant exactly what he said – he planned to see me around. Well he would never see me again, if I could help it.

"He seems like a nice guy," Kenny said..

"He's all right, I guess. He's Kyla's friend," I emphasized.

"Well, Kyla needs to keep him away from Jefferson."

I frowned. "Why?"

"'Cause," Kenny lowered his voice. "I think the guy is gay."

There was nothing in my mouth, but I felt like I was choking. "Excuse me?"

"Come on, where's your gaydar? Didn't you see the way he looked at me? The way he said he would've remembered me if we had met?" Kenny chuckled. "Trust me. Men know gay men."

Men didn't know jack! But what was I supposed to say? Could I tell him that he needed to trust me – that that man was far from being gay?

Of course, I couldn't say that. And it was cool with me, actually. Let Kenny have those thoughts. This way, he'd never get close to the truth of me and Roman.

Kenny would never have any questions about Roman now. All of the questions about that man would be left up to me.

Chapter 9

From the moment Kenny and I left Venice Beach until we finally returned to the Ritz last night, I tried my best to get back into a honeymoon state of mind. And Kenny made a gargantuan effort too.

We walked back into the room. Kenny had worked things out with the hotel staff to have it decorated with rose petals that met us at the front door and led straight into the bedroom. Inside the bathroom, the Jacuzzi tub was already bubbling and waiting for us.

But even though I could see every bit of Kenny's effort, there was nothing I could do to change my heart.

"Jasmine, what do you want from me?" Kenny asked as I moped over the dinner that he had arranged for us to have out on the balcony. This wasn't just any dinner. Kenny had filled the table with all of my favorites: a surf and turf feast that would've rivaled any five star restaurant and a chocolate lover's dessert tray with everything from Godiva mousse to a four-layer German chocolate cake.

Still, none of that could erase the fact that when I looked out the window, the gorgeous view of the marina was a scene I could see from my window at work every day. Nothing would take away the fact that I was honeymooning at home.

"So you don't think you can enjoy any part of this?" Kenny asked.

"I don't know."

"Just because we're in Los Angeles?" he asked, as if that concept was completely unbelievable to him.

I waited a moment to gather my thoughts. To find the right words. Because I felt that I owed Kenny an explanation, at least.

I said, "This dream began for me when I was just a little girl, Kenny. Kyla and I would play together all the time — 'Wedding Day' is what we called the game." I paused as I thought about the way Kyla and I would take big white towels from the linen closet in Kyla's house and tie them around our waists. Instant wedding gowns. "Part of our game, our dream, was where our husbands would take us on our honeymoon. Kyla had heard of a place called Tahiti, and she never let go of that dream." I had to shake my head a bit as I thought about how, almost twenty years later, Kyla's dream had come true when Jefferson had taken her to Tahiti for their honeymoon. "I didn't have a place in mind," I said. "I just dreamed of beaches, and mansions and palaces." I paused again and looked straight into my new husband's eyes. "Maybe that's why I'm here. I'm home because my dream wasn't big enough." Turning away, I peered over the balcony and took in the nighttime view. The marina glimmered with lights from the yachts and the restaurants that sprinkled the peninsula.

Kenny reached across the table and wrapped my hand in his. I didn't look at him. I didn't pull back either.

We sat together, in the silence of the Sunday night, for what felt like hours, but was just a few passing minutes. I knew Kenny was pondering my words and there was a part of me that hoped what I'd said would make him scoop me up into his arms, carry me to the airport, and jet me off to some faraway place.

He broke the silence. "Do you want to just go home?"

So much for my dreams. I needed to just accept the fact that this was the best that Kenny had to offer me.

"No." I shook my head. "That would be worse." Tossing my napkin onto the table, I pushed my chair back. "Give me a little time to work this out. I hope I'll be fine...really. I'm going to try my best. I'll feel better about this in the morning."

As I tried to slip past Kenny, he grabbed my hand. "I love you, Jasmine."

"I know," I said, looking down at him.

"I want to make you happy."

I nodded, but I still left him on the balcony alone. Inside the bedroom, I laid down on the bed, exhausted from this first full day of being married. Was it always going to be like this? A part of me felt a bit like a brat, felt like I shouldn't give Kenny a hard time about this because this was the best he could do.

Maybe that was the problem. Maybe Kenny's best would never be enough for me. I knew for sure he did love me, and it was clear that he'd tried. But for him to think that I would be excited about being home for my honeymoon just showed that the man I'd exchanged vows with didn't know me at all.

But I couldn't blame him for that because maybe I didn't know myself.

How could I not realize that Kenny and I were a long ways away from the college couple that we used to be? While he had been in college handling issues that college boys had to deal with, I'd been dealing with men – men with money and power. Maybe that was the problem. Maybe that was why I couldn't go back to the ordinary. Because this – being in this hotel – was nothing more than ordinary. And "ordinary" was not an adjective I ever wanted in my life.

I closed my eyes, glad that Kenny hadn't followed me inside and praying that he would stay out of the bedroom until I'd fallen asleep. Sleep was all I wanted right now. To sleep and dream about what might have been.

The next time I opened my eyes, daylight was beginning to peek through the window. That was a bit of a shocker; in my head, it didn't feel like more than thirty minutes had passed. I stayed in place for a moment, not wanting to disturb Kenny. His arm was around my waist and I was pressed up against him, my back to his front. At least we slept like a happily married couple.

Except for the fact that I was still fully dressed in the outfit I'd worn yesterday.

Gently, I peeled myself away from Kenny's arm and once freed, I rolled over to face him. Like me, he was still fully dressed. I guessed he'd come in to lie down with me and had fallen asleep, too.

I didn't want to wake him; there was no reason to make him get up now. After all, what could he possibly have planned for today? A trip to Disneyland?

I shuddered and pushed myself from the bed.

Inside the bathroom, I doused my face with water, brushed my teeth, then tiptoed out of the bathroom and bedroom, grabbing my purse from the living room. When I closed the door to the suite behind me, I wasn't sure where I was going – a walk along the marina, maybe. I just needed something that would clear my head, that would help me settle down and realize that Kenny was a good man, and a good man was going to have to be good enough for me.

The hotel's lobby was even grander in the early morning without the hustle and bustle of the guests. With just one suit-clad guy behind the front desk, it was hard not to appreciate the hotel's grandeur. Elegance was in every space of this place, from the sparkling marble that adorned the floors and the walls to the oversized crystal chandeliers that glittered as the early morning sun shone through the stained glass dome ceiling. For a moment, I thought about just settling in the lobby, soaking up this exquisiteness. Maybe in the center of this splendor, I could find a way to appreciate the fact that this was where my husband wanted to spend our first week of life together.

But what I needed most was air. I needed to get outside and walk off some of this tension that had taken root and was growing inside of me. Reaching down into my purse for my sunglasses, I pushed through the glass door and bumped right into someone.

"I'm sorry," I said, looking up. My heart became a jackhammer. "Roman!"

"Jasmine!" he exclaimed as if he was just as shocked to see me.

"What are you doing here?" we said together.

But I wasn't about to fall for his act. He knew what I was doing here. Kenny had told him yesterday.

So, I repeated, "What are you doing here?" because he was the one who had no reason to be in this place.

He grinned. "Didn't I just ask you the same thing?"

I couldn't figure out why he thought anything I said was funny. I didn't find humor in this and really, this man was scaring me now. Hanging out at the Ritz this early in the morning? What was he planning to do? Come up to the room where Kenny and I were staying?

That thought scared me, enough to let me know it was time to stop this. I turned around and began my march to the front desk. I wasn't exactly sure what I was going to say to the clerk, but I was going to make sure that Roman didn't get within shouting distance of me and Kenny ever again.

"Where are you going?" he asked, following me.

"I'm going to report you – because it's obvious that you're stalking me."

He must've thought that I was kidding because he had the nerve to laugh. But then as I kept moving, his laughter went away.

"Jasmine, wait. What are you doing?"

I took more steps.

"You've got to be kidding. I'm not stalking you." I was two steps away from the attendant when Roman said, "Please. If you do this, you could mess me up. I'm not stalking you. I'm here for an interview."

The only reason I turned around was because I had to look into his eyes to see if he honestly thought that I was that much of a fool.

"Really," he said.

"You're here for an interview. Here at the Ritz." My questions sounded like statements. "Please, you're gonna have to come up with something better than that."

"No really. Take a look at this." He pulled an envelope from his pocket, then unfolded the paper that had been inside.

I didn't know why I was even entertaining this crazy man; it had to be my natural curiosity. Tentatively taking the paper, I scanned it.

As I read, he spoke, "I was really impressed with this place when I came here the other day," he said as if he owed me an explanation. "So I checked out the spa and asked if they had any personal trainers. The manager said that was something they were considering and she scheduled an interview with me this morning."

My eyes took in every word of the letter and I couldn't believe it. His explanation lined up with the letter I was reading from a Lolita Carter. Like he said, he had an interview scheduled for this morning. It was the last lines that caught my attention:

I cannot tell you how much I'm looking forward to meeting with you. (I bet she was, especially with a name like Lolita.) You're the kind of man who could add to the Ritz Carlton staff.

Add what?

Then I asked myself why did I care? Whatever, she could have him.

He said, "So you see," he pulled the letter from my hand, folded it back into the envelope and tucked it inside his pocket, "I'm not stalking you."

Okay, so he had a reason to be here, but it still didn't make complete sense. It still didn't feel right. "How did they schedule the interview so fast? You were just here Saturday."

He shrugged. "I know. I was surprised too. This letter was waiting for me when I got home last night. It looked like it had been personally delivered."

I had more questions for this man, like why had he shown up, uninvited, to my wedding. But since I didn't want to get into a long drawn out discussion with him, all I asked was, "Your interview is this early?"

"I want to make a good impression."

He had an answer for everything. Just like a stalker. At least, that's what my intuition was telling me. But then, he did have that letter from Lolita....

"So, you're not gonna turn me over to the stalker police?"

He grinned and I smirked; I had no intention of answering him. In fact, I had no intention of entertaining any further conversation.

As I moved past him, he reached for me, and the feeling of his fingers on my bare arm sent electrical memories through me. There was no other way to describe it – it was like a power surge, from my toes to my head, reminding me of all we had done. Of his hands, his mouth, our union.

I closed my eyes, trying to force it all away.

"What's the matter?" he whispered, his breath heating my ear.

I twisted around, looked up, and his lips were right there. Just waiting for me. Then, over his shoulder, I saw the desk attendant, his curious eyes staring at us. Maybe that was why when Roman took my hand and led me from the lobby, I followed.

We should've been going the other way. I should've made him take me outside, where we would've been in public and I would've been safe. But he led me back down the corridor through a hall that I'd yet to explore but which Roman seemed to know. Wordlessly, I followed, though I was saying all kinds of things to myself in my head. I couldn't go with this man. For what purpose? I didn't want to talk to him. I didn't want to do anything with him.

Moments later, we were back in the area that housed the spa. As he held my hand, I followed Roman inside a men's restroom.

"What..."

But not another word came out of my mouth. Roman pressed me inside a stall and before he closed the door behind us, his lips were smothering mine.

I wanted to fight him. That's what I was supposed to do. But I had no energy – at least, no energy for that kind of battle. Instead, I fought to devour him with my lips, with my hands.

I ripped his shirt from his chest and groaned as I fondled the muscles that were familiar to me now. I assaulted him with every part of my body. My lips, tongue, hands were all over him, and he was all over me. He yanked my skirt up to my waist just in time to enter me and we both moaned with complete joy.

For a millisecond I thought about the fact that just a few floors above, I had a new husband who by now could be awake and wondering about me. But that thought was fleeting because Roman was over me, on me, in me.

It was a cacophony of feelings that I released – frustration, anger, hurt – and Roman turned all of that tension into pleasure. He held me like he understood, he kissed me like he would make it all better, and then he sang in ecstasy with me, his harmony in tune with my melody. And we sang a long, moanful song that ended with notes that could have shattered glass.

Long seconds passed before I was able to move, before my breathing settled. My eyes fluttered open and Roman's face was right there, right in front of me. The skin on his head glistened and perspiration dripped from his face. His breathing matched mine – short quick breaths, that finally slowed. My legs were still wrapped around his waist and his arms were still around me.

Slowly, his lips spread into a wide grin that made my heart pound.

I was terrified. The look in Roman's eyes let me know that I'd just entered into a covenant with a mad man.

Chapter 10

I couldn't get my hands to stop trembling. What had I done? What kind of woman had sex with another man while she was on her honeymoon?

All I wanted to do was cry, but I had to pull myself together. I smoothed down my skirt, checked my blouse and just as I was about to put the key in the door, the suite door swung open and Kenny stood there with wide eyes.

"Jasmine!"

I couldn't help it: I burst into tears.

"Oh my God!" Kenny said, pulling me into his arms. "I thought you had left. I thought you had left me."

"No, no!" I cried into his arms. "I'm so sorry. I'm so sorry!"

Somehow, Kenny pulled me into the suite and he closed the door behind us even though his arms stayed wrapped around me. We held onto each other in the living room, and then suddenly, I pulled back. Suppose he smelled Roman on me?

"Jasmine, I'm so sorry," he said as he wiped a tear from my eye. "I had no idea that planning this – that staying here in Los Angeles – would make you so unhappy. Really, I thought this would be wonderful. I thought our honeymoon would be great and...."

I pressed my fingers against his lips, stopping him. "No," I shook my head, "I'm the one who's sorry. I never should've acted this way." Of course, Kenny had no idea what I was really apologizing for, but I meant what I said from the bottom of my heart. I was so sorry. I never should have been with Roman.

He said, "I guess I really should have talked to you about this first."

"I really should've been just grateful, baby. You were right. All that matters is that we're spending time together."

For the first time in a while, Kenny grinned. I wanted to smile with him, but I couldn't because of all of the regret in my heart.

"So," he began, "does this mean that we're going to have a fabulous honeymoon?"

I nodded, but when he reached for me again, I stepped back because I knew he wanted to seal his words with a kiss. And I couldn't kiss him. Not yet.

When he frowned, I kissed the tip of my fingers then once again, pressed my fingers against his lips. "We're going to have a wonderful honeymoon," I said, trying to keep my voice from shaking. "But first, I have to...take a shower."

His grin was back. "No you don't." He chuckled. "I'm just as funky as you."

I wanted to cry all over again, because there was no way he was stained the way I was. "I'd feel a whole lot better if I took a shower, Kenny."

"Okay," he said softly.

By the way he said that, I knew he could feel that something was wrong. But I was just as sure that he thought I was still unhappy about staying in L.A., and he wasn't going to push it. I'd just apologized, and my husband would do everything to keep the peace.

As I turned toward the bedroom, he added, "Do you want me to join you?"

There was hope in his voice and I closed my eyes for a second wondering how I was going to explain that I had to be alone so that I could wash all of this filth off of me. With everything I had inside, I smiled when I faced him. "I've been acting like a fool," I said. "I just want some time to really get myself together so that I can be right for you." I paused. "Is that okay?"

"You haven't been a fool, Jasmine. I understand."

It wasn't until that moment that I realized just how special Kenny was. I wanted to fall to my knees and just beg for his forgiveness. But instead I smiled and then rushed into the bathroom.

Closing the door behind me, I slid to the floor and held my head in my hands. I was in a state of shock. Truly. There was no way I could explain to anyone, not even myself, what had just happened.

I'd had sex. With a crazed man. I became an adulterer on my honeymoon.

Who does that?

This was beyond the realm even for me. Especially since I didn't even like Roman. And now, I was scared of him.

I sat on the floor with my knees pulled up to my chest for a long time, trying to figure this all out. But time didn't give me any answers. All I had were the questions.

"Okay, Jasmine," I said, "get yourself together."

I pushed myself from the floor, but when I faced the mirror, I couldn't even look at my own reflection.

So I turned around, turned on the shower, and stripped. Even though the outfit I had on was new and cute, I planned to burn every stitch of those clothes.

When I stepped into the shower stall, I thought about the fact that here I was, once again, in this bathroom, trying to scour away my sins. But no matter how hard I rubbed the washcloth against my skin, I couldn't scrub hard enough to get deep enough. There was no way for me to cleanse my heart.

That didn't stop me from trying, though, and by the time I turned off the water, I felt raw, but free. I had reconciled it all. Maybe I couldn't change what I'd done, but I could make up for it. That's what I was going to do. In every possible way, I was going to make up my infidelity to Kenny.

Stepping out of the shower, I wrapped myself inside one of the oversized towels and tried to figure out my new strategy. There was no way I could have sex with Kenny, at least not today. I'd already violated him in one way. There wasn't any way I was going to let him play second to Roman.

I'd have to come up with something to say. Not that I was too worried. Kenny would understand; as long as I was happy and we were together, that would be enough for him. The challenge was going to be me and all the thoughts that were swirling around in my head.

Like I said, though: nothing I could do about the past. All I had now was my future, and I knew for sure that I would never see Roman again.

When I looked up, I caught my reflection in the mirror again. This time, though, I forced myself to look directly in my eyes. It was still hard for me to smile, but I would be able to soon enough.

Taking a final deep breath, I opened the bathroom door and stepped into the bedroom in search of my husband.

Chapter 11

I moaned slightly, as I stretched. I'd slept well – long and deep. It was so good I didn't want to wake up fully, at least not yet, but I could feel the heat of the morning sun peeking in the windows. Slowly, I opened my eyes.

Instantly, I smiled. Kenny was already awake, propped up on his elbow, smiling down at me.

"What?" I said when he kept staring.

"You're just so beautiful. I could look at you like this all day."

"You know how to make a girl feel good." I covered my mouth to keep my morning breath to myself, but Kenny gently eased my hand away.

"You don't have to do that. We're married now," he said.

I laughed and didn't try to even turn away when he gently kissed me.

We were halfway through our honeymoon and I had to admit, I was having a great time. Not that Kenny had changed a thing. We were still in LA, still at the Ritz. But we'd just spent the last two days in bed, exactly the way Kenny had planned this celebration of our marriage.

The only thing that had changed was my attitude. Behind these closed doors with my husband, I was grateful. So grateful that my life was still intact after what I'd done on Monday.

When I walked out of that bathroom on Monday, Kenny was just lying in the bed waiting for me. I had crawled under the sheets with him, but just like I'd planned, we didn't have sex – I couldn't, I wouldn't. I told Kenny that I wanted to be intimate, but in a different kind of way. I told him that all I wanted to do to was hold him. And have him hold me.

That's all we did. We stayed in bed and held each other. And watched TV. And ordered room service.

We didn't have sex.

And Kenny was just fine with it all.

But then yesterday, it was on. I laid it on so hard that by eight o'clock last night, Kenny was straight comatose. The sex had knocked him out cold. I was pleased. Kenny was happy, and Roman was forgotten.

"So," Kenny said leaning back and taking me away from my thoughts. "What should we put on the agenda today?"

I grinned. "Are you trying to back out on me?" When he frowned, I wrapped my arms around his neck and pulled him close. "I thought you said we were going to spend our whole honeymoon in bed."

Kenny's grin was so wide, I could see every one of his teeth. "You ain't said nothing, but...."

A buzzing sound interrupted Kenny and both of our glances turned to the nightstand where Kenny had laid his watch, his keys, and his beeper. It surprised me when he rolled away from me and glanced at the message on the screen.

"Dang!"

Sitting up, I asked, "What's wrong?"

He shook his head. "I can't believe this."

"What?" My tone must've sounded like I was worried, because Kenny turned to me.

"No, nothing. It's not a big deal. It's just that...." He took a breath and turned to fully face me. "I wanted to surprise you." Another breath. "I know you're not really happy with my job. I mean, I know you think I can do better."

"Oh, no," I said. It was the new Jasmine telling that lie.

Kenny chuckled and held up his hands. "I know we're on our honeymoon, but you can tell the truth. You hate that I'm just an analyst at the Times."

This time, I kept my mouth shut.

"So," he said, "I decided to do something, because I always want to make you proud." He grinned and paused so long, I thought he was waiting for a drum roll or something. "I'm going to get my real estate license!"

He jumped up from the bed, so excited, acting like he was about to do the running man or something. I hated to say it, but I was not impressed.

The thing was, I had much bigger plans for Kenny. Like I said, my plan was that he was going to be a star on the speaking circuit, where he would be able to demand fat fees for bringing his star power to all kinds of events. But then, after a few seconds, I began to think this real estate thing might not be such a bad idea. At least not as a beginning. He was still Kenneth Larson, after all. Maybe his star power would help him sell a house or two.

"Jasmine?"

I had to blink to bring myself back from my thoughts.

"I was hoping that you would be excited."

I smiled. "I am. Good for you, Kenny. You'll be good at it. Actually, you're good at everything." But when I reached for him, he backed away.

"The only thing is that I just got beeped from the Ladera office and I know what it's about. There're some papers I forgot to sign last Friday." He shook his head. "Dang. I didn't want anything to mess with our honeymoon, but...."

"Go on," I said. "Take care of it."

"You don't mind?" he asked sounding kinda surprised.

"No. It won't take long, right?"

"Not at all. I'll just run in and sign the papers and we'll get right back on the honeymoon track."

"Sounds good to me."

"Hey, why don't you come with me? It'll only take me a couple of minutes and when I finish, we can grab breakfast."

I tossed the sheet aside, shook my head slowly, and stretched my naked body filling my husband's eyes with a long view of me. "I'm not going anywhere. I'm going to wait right here and have breakfast waiting for you."

I watched Kenny's Adam's apple crawl up, then down his throat. A second later, he dashed into the bathroom like he was being chased by the police. I laughed, 'cause I knew what my husband was doing. And I was right. In less than five minutes, he was out of the bathroom, fully dressed in a pair of khaki cargo pants and a T-shirt. He was gonna make this trip quick.

Kenny strolled over to the bed and snatched away the sheet that I had used to cover myself. His eyes were filled with such desire as his glance roamed over me that I actually blushed.

Really! I blushed!

I was officially a blushing bride.

Leaning over, Kenny kissed me. "I'll be right back." First it was his eyes and now it was his voice that told me how much my husband wanted me.

I watched him walk out the room and shook my head. I was so in love with that man. I mean, I was really in love. Back in the kind of love that I had for him when we were in college. The kind of love that was in my bones, where I couldn't get enough, where I had to have Kenny all the time. I was so glad about it.

So maybe what had happened with Roman wasn't so bad.

Roman.

I hadn't thought about him for days. Well, actually, I had, but I'd shoved all thoughts of that man aside. I couldn't believe what I had done – the night before my wedding and the morning after. It was kinda like an infidelity sandwich, with Roman on the outside and Kenny in the middle. Just ridiculous!

Like I said, though: maybe it wasn't all bad. Because that madness had drawn me closer to Kenny. Roman had served his purpose and now he was gone. Thank God!

The knock on the suite door made me giggle. As I jumped up, I wondered if Kenny had just forgotten his key or had he decided that he wasn't going to go that office after all. Maybe he couldn't stand the thought of being without me, even for an hour.

I wrapped myself in the sheet, sprinted into the living room, whipped open the door and then froze.

I had just been thinking about him and now he was here. Roman stood in front of me, just grinning.

Before I could say a word, he strutted inside. "I see you're dressed for me."

"What are you doing here?" I hissed.

He glanced over my shoulder and looked into the hallway. "Do you really want to have this conversation with the door open?"

I didn't want to have this conversation at all, but I closed the door. "What are you doing here?" I repeated.

"I came to see you, baby."

My heart was pounding and I knew that throbbing would begin in my head at any moment. "Roman, I am not your baby."

He chuckled like I'd told a joke. "You don't have to pretend. I know your husband isn't here."

Okay, this was scary-weird. But I couldn't focus on the craziness that Roman had somehow been watching us. I had to do something about him being here now. Because what would happen if Kenny came back and saw me standing here, half-naked, talking to this guy?

"You have to go. My husband will be back at any moment."

He shook his head as he sat down on the sofa. "I think we have some time." He crossed his legs like he planned to stay awhile. "I saw him get in the car."

My eyes thinned. "What? Are you watching us?"

"No "us," baby. Just you."

Was that supposed to make me feel better? I wanted to call the police, but I didn't know what Roman would do if I did that. There had to be some other way. "Kenny just went to the...store," I lied, figuring that unless he had this suite bugged or something, he'd believe me. "He'll be right back and...."

Roman held up his hand. "I get it. But I need to talk to you."

"There's nothing for us to talk about."

He shrugged. "Okay, I'll just sit here and we can go back and forth about it."

That's when the throbbing started in my head. "Fine, we'll talk. But not here."

Standing, he nodded. "I understand; so get dressed and we'll go somewhere."

I didn't want to go anywhere with this guy, but my first objective was to get him out of this suite. "I'll get dressed, but you can't wait here. Just leave and I'll meet up with you."

His eyes narrowed. "I'm not playing, Jasmine. We need to talk."

"Okay! Go downstairs, wait for me there."

He strolled toward the door, but before he stepped outside, he turned back to me. "If you don't come down soon, I'll be back."

"Give me ten minutes," I said.

He nodded. It wasn't until I closed the door behind him that I realized that not only was my heart pounding and my head throbbing, but I was shaking all over, so much that I could hardly stand up.

At least I'd gotten him out, but for how long?

I had to get rid of him for good. I wasn't sure what I was going to do, but I dashed into the bedroom to get dressed.

Just minutes before, I thought Kenny had dressed in record time, but he didn't have a thing on me. I don't think two minutes passed before I grabbed the room key and my purse and opened the door.

I still didn't have a plan, but the moment I stepped into the hall and let the door close behind me, I heard, "Psssttt."

I turned and saw just a hand waving to me from the stairwell. Quickly, I glanced around, then rushed to the stairs. And there stood Roman, grinning once again.

"I didn't want to take the chance you'd try to slip out on me," he said. He stepped forward and wrapped his arms around me. "I've missed you, baby."

I wiggled from his embrace, pushed him away, and took two steps back until I was pressed up against the wall. "This is crazy, Roman. You're...."

He frowned. "What? You think I'm crazy?"

No, I didn't think he was crazy. I knew it for a fact. But I also knew that crazy people didn't like the truth. Not that I'd had a lot of dealings with folks like this. Usually, I crossed to the other side of the street when I saw crazy coming my way, but for some reason, I was all wrapped up with this nutcase.

Finally I answered, "I wasn't going to say that you were crazy." I spoke slowly 'cause I wasn't sure how many brain cells this dude was working with. "I was going to say that you have to stop this."

The wrinkles in his forehead deepened. "You didn't want me to stop on Monday morning."

I couldn't believe that he was really going there. "I know, but...."

"The night before your wedding, I had you singing in all kinds of languages."

As if I needed that reminder. "That was then," I said. "And that was a mistake."

He shook his head.

"And it's never going to happen again," I added.

It wasn't until he moved toward me, that I realized how I had backed myself into this corner – figuratively and literally.

"See, that's where you're wrong." He leaned forward and pressed his hands against the wall behind me, trapping me inside his arms. "It is going to happen again," he whispered. "And again. And again. And again."

"Roman." I whispered his name because I'd once heard that if you said a crazy person's name over and over, that calmed them down. "Roman," I repeated. "I'm married."

He shrugged. "So?" Then, he leaned forward and pressed his lips against mine.

Now I knew for sure that Roman was crazy. Because crazy recognized crazy, and I was completely out of my mind. I had to be, because the moment his lips touched me, that electrical shock surged and all I wanted to do was to have this man rip every piece of my clothing off me.

But by the time he nudged his tongue inside to meet mine, I came to my senses a bit. "No!" I was huffing and puffing, "I can't do this. We're not going to do this!"

"Come on, Jasmine. You know you want me."

He ain't neva lied, because all I could think about right now was that body-shivering, toe-curling, hand-squeezing, heart-stopping, mind-freezing sex that Roman had laid on me.

But I couldn't give in to that, could I? I was married, right?

Pushing him away once again, I stepped to the side, this time giving myself room. I could dash down the stairs if I had to.

"Why are you playing?" His tone had gone from lust to loathing in two seconds flat. "I'm not into games."

"Neither am I, and that's why you have to listen to what I'm saying. It was nice, but it is over."

Roman opened his mouth, but before he could say a word, the stairwell door swung open and a security guard who looked like he could've been a defensive lineman for the Raiders towered over us.

"Is there a problem here?" he asked, looking from me to Roman and then back at me.

Can you say embarrassed? "Uh, no. We were just talking," I said.

The guard squinted. "Just talking? We have rooms for that. Are you a guest here?"

"Yes, I am," I said, reaching for the key. "My husband and I are in the bridal suite."

"Oh." Now, he grinned as if he had a newfound understanding. "Well, I suggest that you and your husband go back to your room and handle your business because there are cameras all over the place in this hotel." He pointed up at a little black gadget that hung in the corner of the stairwell.

"*I* was just going back to *my* room," I said, making it clear that Roman wasn't with me.

The guard frowned again. "He's not your husband?"

It was only then that I noticed Roman hadn't said a word...and that he was backing away. As if he didn't want anything to do with this man.

"No, he's not."

I had barely gotten the words out of my mouth before Roman dashed down the steps. The security guard and I both stared over the railing, watching Roman jump down the steps two, three at a time.

The guard took his walkie-talkie from his hip, but before he could put out an APB, I laughed, hoping to distract him.

"He's so crazy," I said, as if the way Roman had ripped out of there was some kind of joke. "My brother could've at least said goodbye, but I guess he didn't want to be late for work."

"Your brother, huh?" the guard said as he tucked this two-way back into its holster. "Well, like I said, there are cameras all over this place, so just be careful."

I nodded and ducked my head. Now I was the one to rush away like I was trying to make some great escape.

Back inside our hotel room, I could hardly breathe. If that security guard hadn't shown up when he did, what would've happened? Would I have given in to that madness?

"No!" I said aloud, because I thought if I heard the word I'd be able to convince myself.

I couldn't figure out what was going on with me. I didn't like Roman and I didn't want to cheat on Kenny. Every time that man touched me, though, I seemed to forget those two facts.

But I was Jasmine Cox Larson. I wasn't going to go down like this. I was the one who was in control.

By the time Kenny came back, my decision was made and I had another plan in place.

When Kenny stepped into the suite and the bedroom, he frowned at our suitcases atop of the bed. I'd already packed everything we owned and I was ready to get the heck out of Dodge.

"What's going on?" Kenny asked.

"Baby," I said. "I have a surprise. We're leaving."

"Leaving?" His shoulders drooped just a bit. "For where?"

"Now don't get me wrong," I said, holding up my hands. "I really enjoyed being here, but after you left, I started thinking that it's been wonderful making love in this room every day, but wouldn't it be great if we could do it someplace else?"

Once I mentioned sex, Kenny stood up straight. "Yeah?" The hope was back in his voice. "Someplace like where?"

"For the next four days," I started as I sauntered toward him, "we're going to be," I wrapped my arms around his neck, "at a bungalow," I kissed him and then said, "in Santa Barbara. We're going to be right on a private beach."

"Oh, yeah?" My words wiped the frown right off his face.

I nodded. "I already have visions of us making love tonight, under the stars, at the edge of the ocean."

Kenny looked at me for a moment longer, then grabbed the first suitcase. "How long is it going to take for us to get there?"

I laughed, but inside I released a long sigh of relief, thankful that Kenny agreed and even more thankful that I would be getting away from here.

The Ritz was all that Roman knew about me. Once we left this hotel, he'd never be able to find me.

"Let's go," Kenny said.

I zipped up my bag and then dropped it to the floor. When Kenny picked up both bags, I asked, "You're not going to call a bellman?"

He shook his head. "Nah, I'm good; I don't want anything to slow us down." He grinned. "I'm ready to get part two of this honeymoon started."

Now, I had never been a praying woman – at least, I hadn't been since my mother died – but right now, I sent up a little prayer to God. If He was listening, I had to thank Him for this idea.

Because now, I was safe. And this little thing that had been going on with me and Roman was over for sure.

Chapter 12

Sixteen days!

I had been married for sixteen sweet days, and that thought made me smile. I really was thoroughly happy being a wife, being Kenny's wife. That man was gentle and kind, considerate and loving.

Yawning, I covered my mouth and then took another sip of coffee from the cup that rested on my desk. But that didn't help: I yawned again. I guess I was just sleepy. I hadn't had too many restful nights since I'd become Mrs. Kenneth Larson. Even though we'd been home for a week, Kenny and I were still having that great honeymoon kind of sex. Well, great may have been an exaggeration, but it was honeymoon sex, and I was in love. Wasn't that enough?

I stood up and strolled to the window. Eight floors below, I watched the traffic crawl along Wilshire Boulevard, even though it was hours after the morning rush.

With a sigh, I allowed myself to wander back to my thoughts, trying to convince myself that loving Kenny and him loving me was enough. That man really did have my heart. But the thing was, he didn't ring my bell the way so many other men had.

The way Roman had.

Roman! Since the last time I saw him, for the last twelve days, every time I had sex with Kenny, I thought about Roman. Three people were in our marital bed; Kenny just didn't know it.

That was a really hard and horrible thing to admit, but I lied enough to know that it didn't make any sense to lie to yourself. The truth was Kenny may have been between my legs, but Roman was all up in my head.

Kenny and Roman. Two very different men.

Now I truly understood the difference between having sex and making love.

Making love to Kenny was a full body experience where my husband touched my heart and my soul. In a strange way, I think it was because of Roman that I was more in tune to Kenny. I was more aware, totally aware to all that Kenny made me feel.

But still, Kenny couldn't touch me the way Roman had. It had only been two times, but Roman had heightened my sensitivities and lowered my sensibilities. He could make me scream with just the brush of his lips. He could make me cry with just a flick of his tongue. And when he took me all the way...I'm telling you, there were moments with Roman when I came close to passing out.

But as intoxicating as that man had been, I had to get him out of my head. 'Cause crazy lovers and loving husbands didn't mix.

Pulling away from the window, I inhaled determination: I was going to stop thinking about Roman. Cold turkey. If I wanted to build a life with Kenny, no one else could be in the equation. Not even an invisible no one. So from this moment forward, no more thoughts about Roman. For real, for real.

With my fortitude in place, I sank back into my chair, but before I could even lift my calculator from my desk, there were two knocks on the door. I didn't say a word about coming in to the person on the other side, but the door opened anyway and my boss sauntered in like she owned the place. So many days I wanted to tell Shelly to get over herself, that she was an employee just like the rest of us, that her last name was Brown and not Carnation. But since I really couldn't stand her and hardly talked to her, I kept those thoughts to myself.

"Is your report ready?" she asked me.

Jutting my chin toward the clock on the opposite wall, I said, "Uh...Shelly, the little hand is on the eleven and the big hand is almost on the three, which means...."

"I know what that means, Jasmine," she snapped. "I know what time it is."

The fact that she would even answer me made that funny as all get-out.

I said, "Well, since you know how to tell time, you also know that my report is not due 'til noon."

She placed one hand on her hip and tossed her hair over her shoulder with the other. "I know what time the reports are due," she said in a tone that reminded me she liked me about as much as I liked her. "But I have everyone else's and you know how I feel about being the best team in our department. Right now, you're the weak link."

Inside, I rolled my eyes, but on the outside, I pasted a plastic smile on my face. "I'll have the report to you by noon."

"Noon today?"

Okay, now see? This witch was just trying to work me. Just trying to make me come out and disrespect her. But I'd been through enough mean-girl moments in my life to just ignore her hate. All I did was smile. "Noon today," I said as sweetly as I could, though my words came out sounding more like a bark.

She waited another moment, like she was trying to think of something else to say, just to get on my nerves. Then she spun around. I watched her sashay away as if she thought she was on some kind of runway. Right when she got to the door, she turned back and said, "Noon, please."

That was it! I was just about to curse her out when my gaze rose over her shoulder. I gasped. I had to hold onto my desk so that I wouldn't fall out of my chair.

"What is wrong with you?" Shelly frowned and stared.

I know I had to be looking some kind of crazy, like I was having some kind of heart attack. I could feel it: my eyes were opened wide, but not as wide as my mouth, I'm sure. And my heart was pounding so hard I was sure Shelly could see it coming through my silk blouse.

But she didn't do a thing. She didn't rush to call 911; she didn't offer me a glass of water. Nothing.

Then she turned around.

"Oh!" Even though her back was to me, I could hear her grin. "Well, hello," she said to the object of my medical alert.

I sat there frozen as Shelly's eyes wandered up Roman and then back down again.

What in the world was this man doing here?

The scene played out in front of me. I wanted to get up and stop it, stop her, stop them. But it took me a moment to garner enough strength to even push myself up. And another two moments for my legs to stop quivering enough for me to walk steady.

Shelly held out her hand to the man who had obviously come here to ruin my life. "I'm Shelly Brown. And you are...?"

Before he could say a word, I wobbled over to the two of them. "He's a friend of mine," I answered for him.

"I know that," Shelly said, not taking her eyes away from the man who'd turned my body and my mind inside-out. "But my mother raised me right. I'd like to address your guest by his name." She smiled as if she was auditioning for a toothpaste commercial.

He chuckled. "Just call me Roman," he said, taking her hand.

"What a beautiful name." She tilted her head. "You know, you look familiar...."

"Uh, Shelly, I'm gonna have to break this up. I have a quick meeting with Roman and I have to get those numbers to you, remember?"

She nodded, but her eyes were still on Roman. "I'm telling you, I know you from somewhere."

What was I going to have to do to get this woman out of my office?

Then she snapped her fingers. "I know. You were sitting next to me at the wedding." She turned to me. "*Your* wedding."

"Oh, yeah," Roman said as if he now remembered her.

"So you're a friend of Kenny's?"

This was unbelievable. Shelly and I were closer to enemies than we were to friends, so why was she all up in my Kool-Aid?

I motioned for Roman to step inside of my office and closed the door (at least I didn't slam it) right in Shelly's face. I was pissed off at my boss, but nowhere near as pissed off as I was at Roman.

"What in the world are you doing here?" I kept my voice low and controlled, but crossed my arms.

"I've missed you," he kinda whined. "Do you know how many days it's been?"

Uh, yeah. Twelve to be exact, but I ignored his question. "How did you even find out where I worked?"

He shrugged. "You mentioned it once. After I didn't hear from you, I looked it up. But," he took a step closer to me, "what does it matter?" Another step. "I'm here now."

He wrapped his arms around me as if I was his and he lowered his lips toward mine as if he planned on continuing the stupidity that we had started. But before he could reach his target, I pushed him away and stepped back.

"Roman!"

"What?" he asked, as if he couldn't figure out why I was upset.

"For one, this is where I work. How did you find out that I worked here?"

"You told me."

I didn't know if that was true or not. I couldn't remember. Hell, I could hardly think now that he was in front of me.

"So I figured since we hadn't seen each other in so long, this would make for some great sex, right?"

The memories of all that we'd done rushed to the forefront of my mind, but then, I shook those thoughts away. What needed to be on my mind was getting him out of here and figuring out a way to make him stay away.

"So," Roman leaned back on the edge of my desk, stretched out his legs, and opened his arms giving me a full frontal view of what he had to offer, "I figured you and I could get in a nooner before we hooked up later."

Okay, it was truly time to call the police. But what would I tell them? That I'd had sex on the day before my wedding and the day after with a crazy man? And that even though he was stalking me, I couldn't stop thinking about having him one more time?

I sighed...a bit from fear, a bit from desire. "Roman, the last time I saw you was supposed to be the last time."

"I don't know why you keep denying yourself."

"Because I'm married," I said, much louder than I'd planned to.

"So what?" He pushed himself up from the desk. "Jasmine, look, I know you've missed me as much as I missed you."

Was this man stalking my brain, too?

"And we had a good thing going there," he said as he strolled toward me. "There's no reason to give this up."

"My reason is that I love my husband."

"What's love got to do with it?" he said, quoting that Tina Turner song from a few years back. He laughed as if that was funny.

I didn't part my lips.

"Ah...come on, Jasmine. You can fight this if you want, but you won't win. We were made for each other."

"No, we weren't."

"We're sexual soul mates."

Roman stood no more than five inches away from me and I could see every muscle that made him a man through the shirt that he wore. All I wanted to do was reach out and touch. Put my hand behind his head and lower his lips toward mine and let his mouth take its journey south.

I shuddered.

"See?" he said, knowing the effect he had on me. "I feel the same way about you." But when he reached for me, I took three giant steps back.

"Why are you being so difficult about this?" he asked.

Unbelievable. "Do you realize how you sound?"

"Like a man who's determined."

"No, you sound like a man who's crazy, Roman," I finally admitted. "I don't want you. I've told you that over and over. It was a one-time mistake."

"It was twice," he corrected me. "And it would've happened again if that cop hadn't come into the stairs and interrupted us. And it would've been more if you hadn't left the hotel."

Maybe it was time to call the police and just take my chances.

"Did you leave because of Kenny?" he asked. "Is he suspicious or something?"

I hated that this man had Kenny's name in his mouth and I decided that I wasn't even going to answer him.

So since I was quiet, Roman spoke. "Jasmine, now that I've found you again, I'm not going to let you go. This will never be over."

"I'm going to say this one last time, and then I'm going to call security: whatever little thing we had is

over, and I don't want you to ever come near me
again."

He bunched his eyebrows together, squinted, and
poked out his lips. The intensity of his stare made me
want to step away from him some more, but I stood my
ground.

Slowly, he nodded, as if my mention of the police
made him slow his roll. "So you're really gonna be like
that?"

I didn't say a word.

After a long moment of thought, he said, "Okay."

I was relieved, but not too much. I didn't know
what "okay" meant in his vocabulary.

"Okay," he repeated, still nodding.

"Thank you," I said. I glanced down at a folder on
my desk. "I have to get back to work." After a few
seconds of silence, I looked up. Roman was still
nodding, slowly, like he was still thinking, still
processing everything that I'd said.

"All right," he said. "All right."

He turned and strolled out of the office. Just like
that. Without even a glance over his shoulder. He just
walked away.

"All right," I repeated his last words. "All right." I
released a deep breath and fell back onto my chair.

Finally.

⌒◦⌒

Roman had energized me.

Or maybe being righteous was what had me
productive. I'd gotten that report to Shelly just a
minute before noon and then got a head start on
several other projects. I worked like I was trying to get
a promotion or something, and by the time the clock

ticked to five, I felt like I'd done two weeks' worth of work in nine hours.

Even though I'd put in a full day's work, I made it my business never to leave the office before my boss (a little secret to success that I'd learned from one of my college professors). That was never a big problem, though. Shelly was always out of there by 5:30.

Now, it was 5:31. First, I called Kenny's office. It didn't surprise me that there was no answer; I punched in our home number.

The phone didn't even ring twice. "Hello," Kenny said.

His voice made me smile, but I kinda sighed, too. Of course, Kenny had been sitting right next to me in that business class when the professor had told us how to make a good corporate impression. But somehow, my husband hadn't internalized a bit of that. When the clock struck five in his office, he was out of there.

That was okay, though. I knew my boo was still going to be a big success. I wasn't sure how far he was really going to go with that real estate thing, but on the speaking circuit, he would be a moneymaking machine who didn't have to punch in and punch out. And with me as his manager, both of us would be working-from-home entrepreneurs.

Just thinking about all the money that Kenny was going to earn made me want to run home and do him.

"Hey, baby," I said. "Guess what?" Before he could answer I said, "I'll be home early tonight."

He chuckled. "My definition of early? Or your workaholic definition of early?"

It was true. Compared to Kenny, I was a workaholic. "I'm on my way home as we speak. Well," I chuckled, "not exactly on my way, but I'm packing up."

"That's what I'm talking about," Kenny cheered.

"And you know what?" I said excitedly. "Let's do something special."

"Sure, we can order in. I'll call Yee's and you can pick it up on your way home. Then we'll make a night of it."

"Okay," I said with an equal measure of cheer, as if Kenny's idea was amazing. I was trying my best to hang in there, but just like his idea that L.A. was a great place for a honeymoon, a "night of it" to Kenny was eating shrimp fried rice and drinking his red, always red Kool-Aid while laid out in front of the TV watching that new *Cosby Show*.

But I was going to work with this for now. It was going to get better. Kenny was going to be better.

"Okay, babe. Call in the order in about ten minutes," I said. "This way, it'll still be hot by the time I pick it up and bring it home."

"Can't wait to see you," Kenny said, as if we'd been away from each other for nine days instead of the nine hours since we'd kissed goodbye this morning.

I melted at my husband's words. What he lacked in ambition, he made up for it in love, and in that instant, pictures snapped in my memory of how Kenny nursed me out of my grief when my mother passed away. This man had nothing but love for me, and in the end, it was his love that trumped everything.

"I love you," I said before I hung up and then gathered my purse and briefcase. I couldn't wait to get home to my husband, to our Chinese food and our red Kool-Aid.

Chapter 13

It was just a little before six on a Monday evening, but it might as well have been the weekend with the way the parking lot had cleared out. There were just a few cars left on the entire top floor of the garage in the spaces reserved for the Carnation employees. If this had been a Monday in December, this lot would've still been full. But this was August, and Los Angelenos still had summer on their minds, no matter the day of the week.

The heels of my pumps clicked against the concrete and echoed through the garage, sounding almost like music. I slowed my step and appreciated the beat, wishing I could do it like that new rapper, Ice-T. I loved that new beat "Six in the Morning." It was all about his life in the hood, and I'd heard that those rappers were making big money just talking about the harsh reality of their lives. Shoot, I had some stories to tell too, but since neither Kenny or I could carry much of a tune, I could forget about singing and just get to speaking.

My thoughts were on the rhythm of my steps, the money I was about to make, and the time I'd spend with my husband tonight...which was why I didn't hear a thing until it was too late.

The footsteps came first, but before I could respond, I felt the hand on my shoulder.

I screamed and spun around; with no time to flee, I was ready for the fight.

My heart was pounding when I faced Roman.

"What the hell are you doing?" I screamed. "Sneaking up on me like that?"

"I didn't sneak up." He held out his hands and looked around. "It's broad daylight. I wasn't sneaking anywhere."

"What are you doing here? I told you..."

"I know," he said, not letting me finish. "That's what I want to talk to you about. I want to talk about us."

I put my key in the lock and opened my car door. "Nothing to talk about." I tossed my briefcase and purse inside the car.

He said, "But you never gave us a chance."

I threw up my hands because this was getting ridiculous. "What chance, Roman? I'm married," I said, thinking that he obviously needed that reminder.

"But I was thinking...you could get a divorce."

My eyes widened. It was like I was seeing this cat for the first time. He was absolutely certifiable.

"Let me make this perfectly clear." I paused, giving his brain time to settle down so that he could truly hear my words. "I love my husband."

Roman took a step closer to me. "No, Jasmine. You love me."

What? I opened my mouth, but then shut my lips. My father taught me a long time ago that it was a waste of time to argue with a fool.

"See?" he said when I didn't say a word. "You can't deny it."

The only good thing about this encounter was that now I wouldn't have to work hard to get this guy out of my mind. Truly, I didn't want anything more to do with him. "I don't know what else to say to you," I turned toward my car. Before I slid in, I said, "It would be best if you stayed away from me."

His eyes got small. "Are you threatening me?"

When he took a step toward me, my heart started pumping just a little bit harder. My eyes scanned the top level of the garage, and though there were still five cars parked, there wasn't anyone else in sight.

I inhaled a deep breath. This was Roman – he was crazy, not dangerous. "I'm not threatening you; I'm promising you."

He grinned as if he was amused by my courage. "You made promises to me before."

I shook my head. There was no need to add anything else. "Goodbye," I said, and turned to get into the car.

He was on me so quickly, so swiftly, I didn't have time to take a breath. He pushed me. I stumbled, and my chest hit the side of my car with a thud.

"Ugh!" I screamed. "Roman!"

I tried to step back, but he had me pressed against the car, his front against my back, his body locking me in place.

"Roman!"

His breath was hot on my neck. "You promised that we would always be together," he said, and tickled my skin with his tongue.

In the past, that little move made me drop my panties, but now, his touch was repulsive. "Get off of me." I squirmed, trying to release his grip, but I couldn't move.

"I can feel you, Jasmine," he said. His hands slid to my chest and pinched my nipples. "I can feel how much you want me," he panted.

"Stop it!" I was shocked at how strong and steady I sounded, even though inside I trembled.

"You want this," he told me. Now, his hands wandered down the side of my body.

I twisted and turned, but there was no place for me to go. I was pinned to the car.

He grabbed the hem of my skirt and yanked it up above my hips.

I screamed, but before my voice could echo through the garage, his hand covered my mouth, choking my cries.

The next moments were a blur that moved at space-shuttle speed and crawled by at the same time. I felt every second pass as Roman pushed my panties aside, then fumbled with his own pants. In another instant, he was inside of me, pumping as if I had invited him in.

"You like this, don't you?" he asked.

I couldn't believe this was happening to me.

"Didn't you tell me this was your favorite position?"

Tears spilled from my eyes.

"All you have to do is remember," he panted. "If you remember," he went on, still pumping, "we can go back to the way we were."

I wept, but the sound of my cries were muffled under the weight of his huge hand that covered half of my face. Hands that had once made love to me. Hands that were now violating me. All I could do was stand there. Take it. Pray that someone would come.

Roman humped me like a dog to the rhythm of the passing seconds. I closed my eyes and tried to take myself away, but there was no escape because I could still feel him. I could still hear him.

The minutes moved on and finally Roman shuddered, grunted, and spilled his seed inside of me. For several moments, he stood stiffly, all of his weight heavy on my back. And then, he relaxed and his hand dropped away from my mouth.

I parted my lips ready to scream. But I was alone. With a rapist. Maybe if I did nothing, Roman would just let me go.

I could still hear each heavy breath that he took as he backed off. I waited a second or two, then stepped back, giving myself enough room to slip into my car. Without looking back, I jumped inside, slammed the door, and locked myself in.

My skirt was still wrapped around my waist. Not that I cared. I had to get out of there. It was hard to steady my hands as I aimed the key toward the ignition, but finally, I revved up the engine and released the brakes. Through my peripheral vision, I could see Roman still standing there and for a moment, I closed my eyes and had a dream: What if I put the car in reverse? What if I hit the accelerator? What if I backed into Roman? Rode over him, flattened his body, and crushed his heart? Would anyone ever know? Would they even care?

But then in the next frame, I had a vision of prison.

So instead of doing what I wanted to do, I did what I needed to do: I drove away, twisting my car down to the fourth level, the third level, the second level, and then the last turn that let me out into the daylight.

When the sun hit my eyes, my mind went blank. I had no thoughts at all. I drove mindlessly through the streets of L.A.: down Wilshire, to LaBrea, past the furniture stores and the plant shops and the video stores like I did every single day.

My trembling hands guided the steering wheel; I just aimed my car toward home.

⁓♻⁓

"Jasmine! What the heck?"

I stopped in the foyer of our apartment, wondering what was Kenny staring at. I mean, yeah, I was a little disheveled, but — and then the thoughts came back. The thoughts and the memories.

"Oh God," I whispered. "Oh, God."

I didn't have enough in me to stand. My knees buckled, but before I could hit the floor, Kenny caught me.

"Baby, what's wrong?" He wrapped his arms around me, held me up, and led me to the sofa.

He held me tight as we sat, and for the first time since I'd left my office, I felt safe. But the video still played in my mind. I could see it. I could feel him.

"You're shaking. What's wrong?" Kenny was frantic. "What's wrong?" he asked again.

I squeezed my eyes shut.

"You have to tell me, baby. What happened to you?"

I knew I had to tell him. But my lips trembled; I didn't have enough in me to say a word.

"Jasmine! What! Happened!"

I opened my eyes, looked up and stared straight into his. There I saw all of his love and his concern.

"What happened?" he whispered his question this time. "You can tell me. You have to."

I nodded and did what I always did to Kenny. "I…I…I saw an accident. And, I think…I think the lady, the girl…I think she…died," I lied. "It was horrible. Awful!"

It took a couple of moments for Kenny to register my words, but then all he did was pull me close once again. "Oh, baby, I'm sorry you had to see that."

I sobbed; I couldn't even tell my husband the truth. Because if I told him this truth, I'd have to tell him the truth of what happened the night before our wedding. And what happened the day after. Kenny hadn't done anything to deserve that pain.

So I lied, and I cried. And Kenny did what he seemed born to do: he held me until I had nothing left inside. He held me until the sun dipped over the horizon. He held me until I said, "I'm feeling better now, and you can't hold me like this all night."

"Wanna bet?"

That made me smile, a little. "Really, I'm better now." I sat up, and the memory of what happened rushed me. I squeezed my eyes shut and shook my head.

"Are you all right?" Kenny asked.

I took a breath and nodded. Opened my eyes and faced him. "I'm fine. I just have to…get all of that out of my head," I said, speaking the first words of truth since I'd come home.

Kenny nodded. "It may take you a little while to get over that."

He had no idea how true his words were.

"Listen," he said, "are you hungry?"

I knew this was his effort to help me to think about something else, to help me begin to forget. "Yeah," I said, even though I couldn't imagine eating a thing.

"Good. Then I'm gonna go pick up the food from Yee's."

"Oh my God. I forgot."

"That's okay. I'll just run over there." He stood up, took my hand, and helped me to rise to my feet. "Are you gonna be all right?" I nodded. "I'll be back in ten minutes," he said.

He kissed me again, then held my hand as I walked him to the door. I locked it behind him, checked it twice, then turned around and faced the empty apartment. What was I supposed to do now? What was one supposed to do after being raped? Especially after being violated and not being able to talk about it.

That part was as painful to me as the crime. Roman had attacked me, and I would never be able to say anything. He was going to just walk away, and I couldn't stop him.

Because I could never go to the police.

I'd been a stripper, a high-class prostitute, and I'd had consensual sex with Roman. The police would never believe that he'd raped me. How could someone like me be raped?

I took a breath and stepped toward the bedroom. The only choice I had was to forget. I had to wash away all that had happened...and I would start with a shower to get Roman's stench off of my body. After that, I would work on getting what had happened to me out of my mind.

The moment I stepped into the bedroom, the telephone rang, and I knew right away who was on the other end. This was just like Kenny – to check on me even though not even five minutes had passed since he'd left.

"I'm fine," I said, the moment I picked up the phone.

"You certainly are, Jasmine. That's just one of the reasons why I love you."

My mouth was open, but no words came out. I stood frozen, shaking.

"I'll see you tomorrow, baby," Roman said. "Bye."

And then he hung up.

I dropped the phone like it was a snake and watched it bounce against the carpet. Slowly, I sank onto the bed. Had the man who'd raped me just called and spoken like we were going to hang out tomorrow? How had he gotten my number?

Well actually, that was easy enough. He'd called 411 Thank God I was listed with just a number and not an address. But still, he knew more about me now. What did that mean? Was he going to find a way to come after me again?

The thought made me tremble, but I shook my head. Stood up. No, I wasn't about to just sit down and take this.

I had no idea what I was going to do, but there was one thing I knew for sure: that man was never going to touch me again. Never! No matter what I had to do.

Chapter 14

I felt like I was in hiding. Although I wasn't too much undercover. I was hiding in plain sight: right in my home. This was the safest place for me; even though Roman had my telephone number, I had to believe that he didn't know where I lived.

The sound of the running shower let me know that I had at least a few more minutes to come up with another excuse for Kenny. I had to tell him something since, once again, I wasn't going into work. Yesterday, I'd told him that I wasn't feeling well. I guess today was going to be an extension of that lie.

When the shower stopped and Kenny stepped from the bathroom into the bedroom with water drops still glistening on his chest and a towel draped around his waist, I was ready.

"Morning, babe," Kenny said as he leaned over the bed and then gave me a hug. He sat on the edge when he asked, "Feeling better?"

I kinda nodded and shook my head at the same time. "I'm okay. But I think I'm going to take one more day off."

Kenny bobbed his head in a nod as if he completely understood. He waited a few moments before he said, "That accident really affected you, didn't it?"

"Yeah." I paused as if the accident that I'd lied about was on my mind. "I just need a mental health day."

He smiled. "Mental health. I like that." He stood and moved across the bedroom. "Not quite a sick day, but you're still not well enough to go in."

As he dressed inside the closet, Kenny kept talking, but his words and his voice never made it into that space where I could hear him.

It had been about thirty-six hours since I'd been raped. It was a hard thing to say, but I'd been raped.

Roman had wanted to have sex with me. I'd said no, I'd fought him, and he'd taken me anyway, one hundred percent against my will. So that was the definition of rape, right? It didn't matter that I'd known him and had cheated with him. He was still the criminal and I was still the victim.

But the thing was, there was no one who would believe me. I had no bruises, no cuts, no scrapes. And this man had been my honeymoon lover; who would ever believe that this was rape?

I rolled over to Kenny's side of the bed as if lying where my husband had laid his head would change my perspective. But whether I was on my left side or my right, this was still all so wrong. I'd never be able to convince anyone and even if by some small miracle I was able to do that, I'd lose my husband when the entire truth came out.

I sighed. Talk about sleeping in the bed you'd made. I'd made this one and all I could do was lie in it, alone.

"Babe?"

I had to blink a couple of times to bring Kenny back into focus.

"I've been calling you; you looked like you were a million miles away."

"Sorry. I was just thinking about...the accident."

He frowned as he strolled toward me, now fully suited up. "Do you think you're gonna need to talk to someone about this?"

"What? Are you talking about a psychiatrist or something?" I laughed, though it sounded more bitter than sweet.

"That's what I'm thinking, babe. I mean, this accident did affect you in a way that nothing else has. I'm starting to get a little worried."

I nodded. "It was just...that the accident happened...right in front of me." I looked away when I said, "It was like it was happening to me when I saw that girl die."

Kenny hugged me again because that's just what he always did. "You're safe, Jasmine. You'll always be safe when you're with me."

I closed my eyes to block the tears that I felt rushing forward and I held him tighter. Was it possible to feel innocent and guilty at the same time?

He kissed my forehead, then told me that he'd be home by 5:30, as if he needed to say that. I knew exactly what time that he'd be home. My husband, Mr. Dependable. I'd mocked the trait before, but being attacked had given me new marital clarity. Dependable was the kind of husband Kenny was, and that was the kind of wife I was going to be.

Another kiss, then he said goodbye before he sauntered into the living room. It would take Kenny about two minutes to stop in the kitchen, grab a yogurt drink, and gather the briefcase that he always packed the night before and leave by the front door. I counted the seconds in my head. Sure enough, by the time I got to sixty, the front door opened, then closed.

The lock clicked, but still, I jumped from the bed, dashed into the living room and checked the door twice. Then I checked out the windows, making sure they were all closed and locked. Yes, we lived on the third floor, and yes, it was going to be eighty-five degrees today. But Roman was a special kind of crazy, and since I couldn't tell anyone anything about what was going on, I had to take my own precautions to stay safe.

Not that I really thought Roman was going to appear. I hadn't heard from him at all yesterday — hadn't heard a thing since he'd made that call to me the night before last. My thoughts were that he'd done his dirt and now he'd slither on to his next victim.

But I still had to act in my just-in-case mode.

Once I felt safe, I strolled into the kitchen for a glass of orange juice. Yesterday, I'd spent the day in bed wrapped beneath the covers, waiting for that call from Roman to come. By the time I'd crawled out of bed just fifteen minutes before Kenny came home, I realized I had wasted my day. So after yesterday, I wasn't going to give Roman my today. He'd gotten away with a crime, but he wasn't going to get another moment of my life.

I grabbed the new Essence from the stand in living room where our mail piled up and returned to the bedroom. I'd told Kenny that I was taking a mental health day, and I meant it. On my agenda: relax, relate, release. Just chill and meditate. And after I'd done that, I was going to expunge every memory of Roman from my mind.

Inside the bedroom, I climbed back into my bed and then picked up the telephone. There was one thing I had to do before my mental health day began.

I dialed the number, and when my assistant, Laverne picked up, I put on my best stuffed nostrils/sore throat/congested chest voice.

"Laverne," I said, barely recognizing myself. "I'm still not feeling well."

"Gosh, you sound terrible. Even worse than yesterday."

"I'll be in tomorrow, though."

"Are you sure?"

"Yes." And then I coughed for good measure. I said, "Definitely. Is there anything going on that I need to know about before I head back in there?"

"No, just about everything has been quiet on the home front, except...."

She paused. "You've been getting these calls."

The hairs on the back of my neck were already at attention.

She said, "You had five calls, all really weird, but I wrote down every message."

Calls? What... calls?" My too-sick-to-come-to-work voice was gone.

"Well, the first one came in yesterday at about eight-thirty right after you called in and all *he* said was, 'Tell her Roman called.'"

I noticed the way she put a special emphasis on *he*.

"Then," Laverne continued, "he called back every two hours – exactly every two hours. Like calling you was his job or something."

I wanted to stop the conversation right then. I could hear the curiosity in Laverne's tone, and I needed to nip this now. But I didn't stop her, and she kept going:

"Every time he called, he said something crazier. Like, 'Tell her the Roman Empire has risen.'"

What?

"Then next," my assistant kept on, "he said, 'Tell her the empire will never die.' And when he called again, he said, 'Tell her the empire strikes back.' I almost called security."

"No," I said, talking even though I was holding my breath. "Don't call security. Don't call anyone. He's just...a friend...making jokes."

"Jokes? None of it was funny. He sounded pretty scary if you ask me."

"He's okay; really, he is," I tried to assure Laverne through my trembles. "Has...has he called today?"

"No, but if he does, what do you want me to tell him? Should I tell him that you're home?"

"No!" I shouted. I really wanted to tell Laverne to tell Roman that I'd moved out of the country and was never coming back. But instead I said, "Just...tell him that I'm taking a few days away. With my husband. And that I won't be back for a while."

"Oh...kay," Laverne said slowly after a moment of silence. "Jasmine, are you sure that everything is okay with this guy?"

"Yes." I didn't even bother to return to my sickly voice. The way my blood pressure had shot up was enough; now I sounded sick because I really was. "Roman is just a friend. We like to joke with one another, and we like to...." I stopped. I'd given her enough of an explanation. "Just tell him what I told you to say."

I could hardly breathe by the time I hung up. It had been naive of me to think that Roman had really gone away. I guess in my heart, I never truly believed that. That's why I'd stayed home. That's why I was locked up in this apartment like it was Fort Knox.

Pushing myself up, I paced back and forth, going from one side of the bed to the other, trying to figure this all out. There had to be a way to stop Roman; there had to be something that I could do. But what? Go to the police? No! Tell Kenny? Triple no! Still, I couldn't let him torture me like this. How long would it go on?

I thought and I wondered. I paced and I pondered. Then, I got up the nerve to do what I had to do. In the back of my closet I found the box with all of my souvenirs - jewelry and other trinkets. Gifts from my...dates...over the years. And underneath it all was the shirt that Roman had given me.

Why I had kept it, I don't know. I hate to think that maybe somewhere, subconsciously, I wanted to hook up with Roman again. Or maybe it was that subconsciously I knew I would need his number someday. Well, I was glad to have this shirt right about now, even though I trembled as I thought about what I had to do.

It took me a moment when I went into the bedroom. I sat on the edge of the bed, stared at the white T-shirt, then snatched the telephone, and dialed the number before I could change my mind. On the other end, the phone barely rang once before he answered.

"I've been waiting for your call, Jasmine," he said without saying hello.

How in the heck did he know it was me? This guy was getting scarier by the minute. "Roman," I said his name calmly, even though the memory of what he'd done made anger boil inside of me. "This is it. No more calls, no more visits, nothing."

"I don't think so, Jasmine. I would've thought by now that you'd know we would always be together."

My anger burst into rage. "Do you remember what you did to me?"

"What?" His tone was so full of innocence that for a moment, I wondered if what happened, really happened.

"You know what," I said. My jaw was so tight, it was hard to get my words out. But I was clear; he heard me. And to make it clearer, I added, "You. Raped. Me."

He raped me again when he laughed. "Is that what you call it? Call it what you want, sweetheart. Having sex, making love, rape, it's all the same to me. Whatever you want to call it is fine with me."

I needed to end this phone call before he heard my tears or sensed my fears. So I took a deep breath and said, "You don't want to mess with me," in a tone that held all kinds of threats.

"No, Jasmine," he said in that voice that he'd always used when we were having sex. "You're the one who doesn't want to mess with me." A pause. "Look, let's just get together tonight and talk about this. Obviously, you're upset about something...."

I had to pull the phone away from my ear to stare at it for a moment. Really? Did he think that I was upset? Really? Did he think that we were going to get together? "That's not going to happen," I said, pressing the phone back to my ear.

"Let's just meet tonight," he kept on as if I hadn't spoken, "and we'll work it out." "This is the very last time that I'm going to say no, and it's the last time that we're ever going to speak."

When he paused, I thought that I'd finally gotten through to him.

"Well, if you won't talk to me," he said at last, "maybe Kenny will."

Those words were like a stab to my heart. "I'll just give Kenny a call and see if he wants to meet with me. I have lots to say and I'm sure he'll listen."

I had no doubt that Roman meant every word that he said, but what was I supposed to do? Meet him? I couldn't, I wouldn't. So, I came back strong, "You go to Kenny, and I'll go to the police."

"Really? And what will you tell them?"

"That you raped me. If you go to Kenny, I won't have anything to lose."

In the second that he hesitated, I knew that I stood a chance.

"No one will believe you," he said. "We were lovers."

"Try me and we'll see. And you better pray that you're right or else you're going to jail." I didn't wait for his comeback; just hung up because there was nothing left to say, and because I was trembling so much it was difficult to hold onto the phone.

Falling back onto the bed, I sat still, just listening to my breathing for minutes. I'd been in lots of fights in my life, and you could count on one hand the number of fights that I'd lost. But this wasn't a fight; this was war. Roman wasn't battling with his hands. He wasn't even holding a gun. He was at war with missiles while I was trying to stab him with a knife.

There was no way I could win, but that wasn't going to stop me from trying.

My day of relaxation was shot.

From the moment I hung up the phone from Roman, I'd been beyond afraid. Was he really going to call Kenny? Of course he would. Making a call to Kenny was nothing compared to what he'd done to me. My only hope was that he'd taken my threat seriously. I didn't have much hope for that, though. You had to be sane to be serious, and Roman had already shown me that he had no personal relationship with sanity.

So what was I supposed to do now? Keep Roman away from Kenny? How? That would be a daunting, 24/7 task. I'd have to be with Kenny every hour of every day, and that could never happen.

I'd have to handle this day-by-day, hour-by-hour, really. And I'd have to start now.

Picking up the phone, I planned my words. My goal was to keep Roman and Kenny apart, but I had to have a back up just in case Plan A didn't work. I had to prepare Kenny for what might come.

"This is Kenny Larson," my husband said into the phone on his end.

The sound of his voice brought tears to my eyes. I know I didn't always act like it, but I really did love this man. It was more than all the time and effort I'd put in to make him my husband – it was about the way he loved me. There would never be another man who would love me so unconditionally, and I had to do everything I could to keep him.

"Hey, babe, it's me," I said.

"Hey, what's up?" he asked. I could hear the surprise in his voice. I never called Kenny during the middle of the day. In the next second, he asked, "Is everything okay? Are you all right?"

I swallowed. "Yeah...I just wanted to hear your voice."

"Ahhh, that's sweet. You've never said that before."

"I know." I let a beat go by. "Kenny, there are a lot of things I've never said before. Like how much I love you."

He chuckled. "I've heard you say that a time or two."

"No really. How much I really love you. How much you mean to me. And how I would just die if I lost you."

I could hear the frown in his voice when he said, "Jasmine, are you sure that you're okay?"

It was a shame that telling my husband how much I loved him made him think that something was wrong. I guess he was more used to me complaining, trying to nag him into being a better (richer) man.

"Yeah, I'm okay. It was just that I've been thinking a lot about how wonderful you are and...." I had to pause. "And sometimes I don't know if I deserve you."

"That's how I feel about you, babe."

"I'm not the most perfect person, Kenny, but I want you to know that no matter what, I love you, and I'm going to get better, okay?"

"Sweetheart, no one is perfect, and I love you just the way you are. I will always love you. Forever. For always."

If his words were money, I would take them to the bank and make that withdrawal once Roman blew up our world.

"Jasmine, you know that, right?"

If his words were money, I'd be able to tell him the truth. But even though Kenny meant what he said right now, his words were just words. His heart would be broken if Roman told him what had been going on and after that, there would be no way that he could love me forever, for always.

"Are you sure you're okay, babe?"

I hadn't even felt my emotions pouring from my eyes until the first tear dripped from my cheek onto my hand.

"Yeah," I sniffed. "I'm okay. It's just that...we're just getting started...and...I really want to do this marriage thing right."

He chuckled. "We'll wade through this together. We'll get it right, together. You don't have a thing to worry about. We're in this for better, for worse, together. All right?"

Even though he couldn't see me, I nodded. "Yeah."

"For the next fifty, sixty, seventy years, okay?"

"Okay."

"Listen Jasmine," his tone had changed from peaches and cream to all business and I imagined that someone had stepped into his cubicle. "I've got to go."

He hung up without really saying goodbye and it took me a couple of seconds to realize that he was gone.

I stood there, just holding the phone in my hand. Nothing had been accomplished in my quest to keep Roman away from Kenny, but at least if it all went down tonight, if Roman did contact Kenny, the last words my husband heard from me before his world exploded were that I loved him. Maybe that would be enough.

What I really wanted to do was go down to Kenny's office and sit at his desk and answer every call. But since that wasn't going to happen, I waited at home. Waited for that phone call from Kenny where he would tell me that Roman had done exactly what he said he would do.

From just before eleven 'til noon, I paced the length of the living room. From noon 'til two I paced the width of the bedroom. I went back and forth between the two spaces, doing nothing else. I ignored the TV in the living room and I heard nothing from the radio in the bedroom. The only thing that was on my mind was the scenario that I couldn't stop imaging. It was like there was a VCR in my brain and I kept pressing play. I could see it, I could hear it: Kenny yelling, screaming, calling me all kinds of names. Telling me to be out of the apartment and his life before he got home from work.

Every time I passed the telephone, I stared at it, praying that it wouldn't ring. And every time I passed a clock, I willed the time to pass quickly so that Kenny would come home and be safe here with me.

I was waiting right at the front door at 5:30, when Kenny put the key in the lock. When he stepped inside, glanced at me and then smiled, I fell right into his arms.

"Wow," Kenny said as he hugged me back. "I think I like having you at home waiting for me. I could learn to love this."

"And I already love you," I told him before I kissed him.

We kissed the way we did when we'd first met in high school: as if we were each other's meal.

My plan for the rest of the night was to keep Kenny close to me and away from the phone. And to tell him I loved him at least one million times.

Tonight, I would pray that one million would be enough insurance for what I knew was coming.

Chapter 15

I'd spent the whole next day acting crazy.

But it wasn't my fault – not exactly. It was because of that VCR in my mind again. Playing every scenario of everything that could go wrong. I was a madwoman, and that was a gift from Roman.

Not that I'd heard from him. Last night, the phone never rang. Once again, he was silent. But I'd fallen for that trick before, and I wasn't going to fall again. I knew the silence meant nothing.

Except...

Maybe I had really scared him with my threat to go to the police. Though I wouldn't put a lot of money on that bet, because crazy never scared easily.

Crazy had me scared, though. That's why I'd taken all kinds of precautions from the moment I woke up this morning. Even though I'd decided that Roman wasn't going to keep me in the house for another day, I still couldn't walk around outside as if I were free. My steps were planned, everything I did was measured from the moment I left my apartment for the first time since I'd been raped.

My drive to work was always an uneventful one – I didn't even have to be fully awake since it was just a straight shot down LaBrea. But rape changes things, and this morning, my eyes had been open wide as I noticed every car behind me, beside me, in front of me. My eyes ached from the constant movement, darting back and forth, checking every street corner, every stop light, every bush along the way.

There were no signs of Roman.

Within ten minutes, I was on Wilshire, but I didn't rush into the garage the way I always did, trying to get one of the premium spaces near the elevator. This morning, I edged my car to the curb, shifted into park – though I left the engine running – and waited. My eyes stayed on the entrance to the garage as car after car turned in. I didn't move until I saw one that was familiar: Carol Wilson's red Nissan. I rolled in right behind her, staying as close as I could. On the top level, Carol took one of the assigned spaces and I twisted my car so that I was next to her.

She greeted me with a wave as she stepped from her car before I could even turn off my engine.

I grabbed my briefcase, jumped from the car and did a mad dash to catch up with her. When she frowned, I explained, "I didn't want to wait for the elevator."

"Girl, I understand that. They need to fix this old thing," she said. "I get so tired of waiting forever."

While she chatted, my eyes scoped the space to see if we were truly alone. I tried not to think about the last time I was here, when it was just me and Roman.

When a car rounded the corner a bit sharply and the tires screeched against the concrete, my pulse spiked with fear. But then the red-headed, freckled guy drove past us and waved: Jason, the head of Marketing. Not Roman, the crazy rapist.

I still didn't breathe freely until I was upstairs in my office.

And this was where I'd been ever since, behind closed doors. Not that I felt completely safe here, but at least if Roman showed up, he wouldn't be able to touch me. Not in front of all of these witnesses.

I had returned to work physically, but I hadn't been able to bring my mind with me. Right now, Roman owned that. He owned my thoughts, my time. He was not present, but it was hard to make a move without thinking of him.

And it was hard to work because I called Kenny every twenty, thirty, forty minutes to find out if Roman had destroyed our world.

Even now as I picked up the telephone to make the call, my hands trembled; it didn't matter that I'd spoken to Kenny less than an hour ago.

"Jasmine, what's going on?" Kenny almost whined.

"I'm sorry. Can I help it that I'm a newlywed?"

"I'm one too. But I'm a newlywed who has to work, baby."

"Okay." I paused. "What about doing something special tonight?" That thought just came to me. If Kenny and I were a moving target, it would be more difficult for Roman to find us, to catch us, to destroy us.

"That's sounds great," he said, though I'm sure part of his excitement was to just get me off the phone. "Wanna do dinner and a movie?"

Dinner and a movie – a special night, Kenny Larson style. In the past, I would've been annoyed that he didn't make the effort to be more creative. Today, I was just glad that he'd agreed to go anywhere, do anything.

"That would be great. I'll make the plans and then call you back," I said, glad that I'd have an excuse for the next time I called.

At least I'd have something to do for the next hour or so. I started first with the movie. A couple of weeks ago, I really wanted to see that new film *Fatal Attraction*, but from what I'd heard, it was some crazy-doesn't-want-to-go-away drama and I already had enough of that in my life. So I settled on *Moonstruck* because Kyla had told me that Cher was the real deal in that picture. Next up – where would we eat? If that choice had been left to Kenny, we'd be hanging out in the food court of the Fox Hills Mall trying to decide if we wanted two or three items on the Panda Express menu.

That was not about to happen; I may have been living in fear, but I wasn't about to do it bargain-basement style. I knew exactly where I wanted to go: to that new restaurant, *Georgia's,* over on Melrose. It was the place to see and be seen – a celebrity haven, since it was owned by Norm Nixon, Denzel Washington and a few other Hollywood A-listers. My hope was to see someone, and maybe one of those someones would recognize my husband and help jumpstart his career. But the bigger thing for me is that I knew we'd be safe from Roman. *Georgia's* was exclusive, not a place for someone like Roman to go, since that man didn't have two nickels. Not that we'd ever discussed his finances; money was not the reason that I'd been with Roman.

With the plans in place, I called Kenny back. He didn't even grumble at the fact that I'd chosen a restaurant over the food court, and I promised not to disturb him at work again unless it was an emergency.

I spent the rest of the afternoon shuffling papers, shifting folders from one side of my desk to the other, watching the clock, and shaking every single time the phone rang. By the time the clock slowly ticked to quarter to five, I had one of those good news, bad news scenarios. Starting with the bad: I hadn't gotten a lick of work done. Ending with the good: I hadn't heard from Roman.

I was beginning to think that maybe that man did have a little bit of sense. Maybe the thought of the police tracking him down and then cuffing him up was enough to make him go away. Maybe there was something in his past that made him decide it was better not to test me. Whatever his reason, I was just beyond relieved that I hadn't heard from him.

But had Kenny?

I picked up the phone – again – and held my breath – again – until my husband answered . "Hey, babe," I said. "Just want you to know that I'm leaving the office now."

He laughed. "What? You're not gonna have me sitting at the restaurant waiting for you? You really have changed."

"I told you. I've turned over a new leaf. I'm in love."

"Well, I love this new-leaf-Jasmine. I'll see you in a few, babe."

I dropped the phone back in place and breathed, relieved. It looked like we were going to make it through tonight, at least.

I still had to be safe, though, and for the first time since I'd begun my career, I didn't wait for my boss to leave the office first. My briefcase was already packed and when the clock hit five, I marched out of the office with a slew of Administrative Assistants who never stayed a minute past five. The elevator was packed as I rode down to the garage, and though I wanted to throw up when the doors opened and my eyes surveyed the space where I'd been attacked, at least I knew that this time, surrounded by eight women, Roman wouldn't be able to get anywhere near me.

I trotted to my car, jumped inside, and locked the door before I stuck the key in the ignition. The engine turned over – and only then did I finally feel safe.

My office was closer to the restaurant, so it was no surprise that I was there before Kenny. The moment I tossed my car keys to the attendant and strolled into *Georgia's*, I knew this was just what I needed to make me forget the madness that had become my life, even if it was just for a little while.

The crowd was light. Most of the up and coming black professionals who mixed with Hollywood were still in their offices, working to make a name for themselves, working for those extra dollars to be added to their annual bonuses, all eager to make their mark on the last few years left in the eighties so that they would be major players in the nineties. I understood the ambition; it was in my blood too, and just as soon as I was sure I was safe from Roman, I was going to get back to my workaholic ways so that Kenny and I could have a wonderful life.

"Hello, Ms. Cox."

I grinned and nodded at the hostess who looked like she was barely old enough to work. She must have an amazing photographic memory because every time I came into this place, she remembered my name.

"It's Mrs. Larson now," I said proudly.

"Really?" She smiled, showing the orthodontist-set teeth that had to have cost her parents a fortune. "I didn't know. Congratulations."

"Thanks," I said, as she moved from the hostess stand. I followed her past empty table after empty table to one in the far corner next to the kitchen door.

Was she kidding me? "I don't want to sit all the way back here," I said. I pointed to one of the other tables. "What about there?"

She turned around as if she had to check out what she already knew. "Uh," she said, "those tables are reserved."

I raised an eyebrow.

"We're expecting our regular crowd soon."

I knew that was code for, "That table is for important people." But it didn't stop me from raising both of my eyebrows.

She said, "But maybe I can move you here," in a tone that was meant for me to know she was doing me a favor. She took a few steps, moving two tables away from the first one.

I sighed, but this was as good as it was going to get.

I hung my purse on the back of the chair and sat down. When the hostess walked away, I rolled my eyes, but just as quickly checked myself. There was no need to get upset about a table. Soon enough – once Kenny started his new career – I'd be seated right in the center of the restaurant every time I came in here. It was just a matter of time.

The sure way to pull myself out of this little funk was to glance at the menu, even though I already knew what I was going to order (I loved the barbecue salmon). Still, glancing through the other choices – the shrimp and cheese-grits and the pecan-crusted chicken breast – always tempted me.

"Hey babe."

I heard his smile before I even had the chance to glance up. Every time I saw my husband these days, I was more than thrilled. He greeted me with his crooked smile and that glow in his eyes that told me how much he loved me. The way he said hello let me know that we had at least one more night of happiness.

I grinned and jumped from my chair. Wrapped my arms around him, closed my eyes and held him as tightly as I could. I might not be a religious woman, but I said a little prayer thanking God that another day had passed without Kenny finding out the truth.

I squeezed my husband once more, opened my eyes, and gasped.

Just feet away, behind Kenny, stood Roman – grinning at me.

"Oh my God."

Kenny pulled away and held me by my shoulders. "Baby? What's wrong?"

It was hard for me to breath; Roman was right in my view.

"Jasmine!"

Roman moved a step closer, and his grin got wider. I closed my eyes and trembled more.

"Jasmine? What's wrong?"

I was trying to think, think, think. I had to figure out what to say to Kenny, how to explain this whole thing to him in just seconds before Roman came over and blew up my world.

"Jasmine!" Kenny called out to me again.

I opened my eyes and Roman was just two feet away.

"Baby, talk to me," Kenny said.

That was when I did the only thing that I could do. I closed my eyes and wilted to the floor.

"Jasmine!" Kenny yelled. I could feel him over me as I held my breath. "Oh my God! Please, help me. My wife just fainted!"

Chapter 16

I couldn't believe I was in the back of this ambulance, but here I was, rocking and rolling as the vehicle, with its lights flashing, sped down LaBrea.

"All of her vitals are stable," the EMT said to the other who was driving. "Though her heart rate is still rapid and her blood pressure is still a little high. But there's nothing else."

What else could there be?

That's what I wanted to ask him, but I kept my eyes closed as the EMT took the blood pressure band off of my arm. On the other side of the gurney was Kenny, holding my hand, squeezing it every couple of seconds, and telling me through the whole ride that I was gonna be all right.

When the car slowed down for what I figured was traffic, I peeked through one eye at Kenny. He was looking out the back window, so he didn't see me, but the poor guy was still shaking.

Dang-bang-it! I hated doing this to my husband, scaring him this way. But what else was I supposed to do? Roman had been right there, standing just feet away.

The thought made me groan again.

"Baby," Kenny whispered as he turned back to me, "it's gonna be okay."

He was wrong about that. Roman was serious about ruining my life. This wasn't a game for him; this seemed to be his life's purpose.

And the energy he put into his purpose seemed to be far greater than my efforts to keep him away from us. I was sure that once I'd fainted, he would run the other way. My plan was that someone would think I was dead and that news would rush through the crowd; Roman would hear that, and he would hightail it out of there, knowing that my death was his fault. My blood was on his hands, and he'd feel guilty all of the days of his life.

At first, I thought my plan had worked. After Kenny screamed out that I wasn't breathing, I could hear people shouting. I could feel the energy around me, folks rushing from here to there, getting towels to put under my head and a tablecloth to cover me. Somebody fainting at *Georgia's* was a big deal, and I played it all the way.

The EMTs showed up about ten minutes after I faked the funk, got me onto that stretcher, and then rolled me through the crowd of diners and employees standing around with wide eyes and open mouths.

But as I peeked through my eyelashes, there was Roman! Pretending that he was just another face in the concerned crowd. He stood out, though. How could he not? With that bald head and fine face, and those eyes, not to mention those muscles. But what stood out the most was that while there was not one other person with a smile, Roman was grinning so hard I swear I could see all thirty-two of his sparkling teeth!

Like he knew that I was faking this whole thing. This was a joke to him.

Remembering the way he stood there, taunting me even as I lay on the stretcher, made me groan again. That sent Kenny into his reassurance mode. But there was nothing that my man could say, and no medicine that the doctors could give that would cure me. Roman was going to tell Kenny everything.

What was I going to do?

Thinking about Roman kept my heartbeat up and my blood pressure rising. At the hospital, the EMTs dragged me from the ambulance and across the concrete driveway, hitting every bump along the way. I had a headache by the time I landed in the emergency room. The two men rolled me to a curtained-off section pretty quickly, thank God, and left me alone with Kenny.

I was grateful for that. I didn't want doctors rushing to save me when there were folks in the ER who really needed somebody to save their lives. I would've felt awful if someone had died while a doctor was trying to figure out my fakery.

"Baby?" Kenny's voice was shaky as he stroked my hand, so gently, as if he thought I might break if he applied any kind of pressure.

I let my eyes flutter open. "What happened?"

"You fainted."

"I did?" I said, playing the whole thing out.

"Yeah. We're at the hospital. They're gonna check you out."

"I'm fine," I said. "Really. I'm fine."

But thoughts of Roman made me squirm. I had no idea how he'd known I was at *Georgia's,* so what was to stop him from coming here? He didn't need to do a lot of investigating to figure out where I was right now; leaving in the ambulance was a good clue.

"Baby, are you okay?"

"Yeah," I squeaked, trying to sit up just a bit.

"I'm gonna call the doctor; you're really sweating now."

I hadn't even noticed that, but I wasn't surprised. My thoughts made it hard for me to breathe and my chest was beginning to ache from the way my heart was pounding. Now I needed medical attention for real.

Stepping over to the curtain, Kenny peeked out. "Please! I need a doctor in here. My wife...."

I bounced back on the gurney, too weak to even sit up. I couldn't believe I was causing all of this distress – for myself and for Kenny – just because my panties had fallen off with Roman.

I leaned back and closed my eyes. Either I was gonna have to tell Kenny, or I was gonna have to die. Those were my only options, and they seemed pretty equal to me.

"Mrs. Larson?"

I opened my eyes. The bright light above where I was lying made me squint. I hadn't even heard anyone walk into the room.

A man in a bright white lab coat took what looked like a penlight from inside his jacket and shined it into my eyes, first my right one, then my left. "Can you see me?"

Was this doctor kidding? How was I supposed to see anything with that bright light in my eyes?

I blinked a couple of times after he put his flashlight/weapon away. "I can see now."

He nodded and felt my forehead the way my mother used to when I was a kid. What kind of doctor was he?

"I'm Doctor Avery," he said as his hand ventured across my forehead. "You do seem a little warm, but nothing outside of the ordinary." He pulled over the stool, sat his butt down, looked at me, and said, "Okay, talk to me."

I frowned. "About what?"

"About what's causing this reaction. If I had to guess, it seems like you had some kind of anxiety attack."

If he had to guess? Were doctors supposed to guess anything? I wanted to see this guy's medical degree.

"So tell me," he continued, "what's going on in your life?"

I glanced at Kenny, standing at the foot of the gurney, then lowered my eyes. "Nothing," I whispered.

"Doctor," Kenny began, "we just got married. Someone told me once that that's pretty stressful."

The doctor chuckled. "Indeed it is." He peered at me as if he was trying to see right through me. What kind of doctor was he? I hoped he wasn't one of those new age psychic people who could see into the beyond, like into your thoughts and mind. He said, "Do you think you're pregnant?"

"No!" I said before he could even finish. "No! We just got married."

The doctor chuckled. "Uh, length of marriage doesn't have anything to do with pregnancy." Doctor Avery glanced at Kenny.

My husband grinned. "Do you think...."

"No!" I said. I wasn't really sure it I was telling the truth or not. I mean, I hadn't thought about being pregnant. But being pregnant would be much worse than anything else that was going on right now. Because that would mean that I was pregnant by one of two men.

"So there's nothing else?" the doctor said.

Kenny answered, "Well, there was that accident."

The doctor looked from Kenny to me, and then back to Kenny. "What accident?"

"She saw a really bad accident," Kenny said. "She's been upset about it ever since."

When the doctor turned to me, I figured he wanted me to say something, so I added, "Yeah, I watched a little boy die."

"A little boy?" Kenny frowned. "I thought you said it was a little girl."

My mother had told me that the hardest part about lying was keeping track of the lie. I had to get better at this. I leaned back, closed my eyes and moaned

"All right," Doctor Avery said. He had an extra little lilt in his voice. As if, like Roman, he knew that I was faking. "I'm gonna take some blood, run a few tests, just to be sure. But overall, I think you're okay. Like I said, seems like it's just stress." He patted Kenny on his back before he left the room, as though he felt sorry for him or something.

Could the doctor tell I was lying just by looking at me?

When he left us alone, Kenny turned to me with confusion in his eyes. I knew he was probably still thinking about how the sex of the accident victim had changed. "I agree with the doctor," I said, wanting to give Kenny something else to focus on. "It's stress. All the planning for the wedding. My job."

"Yeah," he said. "Plus it's not all that easy being my wife," he kidded.

That almost brought tears to my eyes. "But being your wife is all I've ever wanted."

He bent down and pressed his lips against mine, but gently. "Just lean back and relax. There's no need for you to be stressed in here."

I did what Kenny told me, but my husband just didn't know. In a few seconds or minutes or hours, Roman could show up and stress me the hell out.

"I'm gonna step out for just a minute. I wanna check with Dr. Avery and make sure he was telling us everything."

I nodded and he kissed me again. He took three steps toward the door before I stopped him. He turned around when I called his name.

"I love you, Kenny."

He grinned as if he already knew that. "I love you too. Just relax."

Outside of my curtained space, I could hear the sounds of sickness all around me: the constant beeps of machines, the chatter of nurses, the strong voices of the doctors shouting orders, making demands. But inside my space, there was peace – for the moment. At least for these next few minutes, however long it lasted, I was going to relax.

I leaned back on the gurney, wiggled until I found a comfortable space, and closed my eyes. I took a deep breath. And then, I groaned.

Because inside my head, all I could see was Roman.

Chapter 17

Kenny walked me into our apartment as if I had really been sick.

"Here, baby," he said when we stepped inside, "let me get you settled on the couch."

I went along with it all – his caring and his loving – because I just didn't know how much longer I was gonna have it. I knew that soon, very soon, this jig would be up. I couldn't keep Roman away from Kenny forever; that was proven today. I just needed to figure out the best way to handle what was to come.

When I leaned back on the couch, Kenny said, "I should've asked if you wanted to go into the bedroom."

"No," I said. "I'll just rest here for a while."

He nodded. "Well, I'm going to fix you something to eat."

"I don't want much. I don't have an appetite anymore," I said, thinking about how I might never eat again.

"The doctor said you had to have something."

"Okay, just some yogurt."

Kenny nodded and kissed my forehead before he left me alone. I just wanted to cry. I had put my life at such risk.

But the truth was, I never thought I was risking a thing. Working at Foxtails had spoiled me. I'd been with so many men, for such a long time, without Kenny – or anyone – finding out. I thought I was invincible. I was the Master Liar. A deceiver at the highest level.

I guess what they say is the true: whatever is done in the dark will always come to the light. And this light was going to put the brightest spotlight on who I was. My whole marriage, my whole life, was a complete lie.

There were tears in my eyes when I pushed myself up on the couch and peered toward the kitchen. I couldn't see Kenny in there, though I could hear him opening and closing cabinets, slamming the refrigerator, running water. That man didn't deserve any of the hurt that was about to pour down on him.

I decided right then that since this storm was coming, it would go down the way I wanted it to. If Kenny was going to find out about me and Roman, it would be best if it came from me. I'd tell him as gently as I could; at least that way, I'd have a chance to explain and tell him just how much I loved him. Then maybe – though, I doubted it – I could save my marriage. Even if there was only a one percent shot, it was better than the chance I'd have if Roman walked up to Kenny and said, "Hey man, thanks for letting me screw your fiancée and wife."

I breathed in the deepest breath that I could, not knowing when I'd have a chance to breathe like that again. I was going to tell Kenny now, before I lost my nerve. This way, I'd have all night to beg him to stay. He wouldn't be able to go anywhere – both of our cars were still at the restaurant. He'd have to stay here and talk to me, or at least listen as I begged for his forgiveness.

"Okay, baby, here's your dinner." Kenny strolled into the living room balancing a tray in both hands.

Although my heart ached, just looking at my husband made me smile. "What's all this? I told you I just wanted yogurt."

"It is yogurt. Banana," he said as he sat the tray down beside me on the sofa. "I just didn't want you eating out of the carton."

My husband had taken that little container of yogurt and made it look like a feast. He'd filled a crystal bowl with the yogurt and had placed a full place setting, with a knife, fork and spoon next to it. In the corner of the tray was a glass of his infamous red Kool-Aid, and next to the glass, there was a small vase with a single flower that he'd plucked from the plastic bouquet in the center of our dining room table.

I looked up at him and prayed that he could see all the love that I had for him.

"Kenny."

He looked at me, waiting for me to say more.

"Kenny," I repeated his name. My lips began to tremble.

And right before I burst into tears, he said, "Oh, baby, don't cry. I know what you're trying to say. I know how much you love me. I love you too. I'll love you forever and for always."

⁓ ✺ ⁓

Forever and for always.

In the darkness, Kenny's words blared in my mind. It had been that way from the moment he'd first said them to me tonight. The words were there even when he pushed the yogurt aside because I couldn't eat through my sobs. The words were there even when he walked me into the bedroom and undressed me as I cried. The words were there as we lay together, as he held me and kissed me and told me that he loved me, too. Forever. For always.

That was when I cried harder. I cried until I was exhausted and Kenny had fallen asleep.

He rested; I didn't.

But even as he snored softly, his words still played in my mind.

Forever. For always.

Those words were so important to him. That's what Kenny had promised when we first became boyfriend and girlfriend; that's what he promised when he proposed; and that's what he promised when we got married.

Forever. For always.

It was his promise, his commitment – and unlike me, Kenny wasn't a liar or a cheater. He meant what he said.

Kenny's hand rested on my waist and gently, slowly, I rolled over in the darkness, careful not to awaken him. I slid out of the bed, covered myself with my robe, and snuggled into the oversized chair in the corner.

I loved this old, soft chair. So broken-in that it was beyond comfortable. From here, even in the dark night, I could see the tip of the downtown skyline that wasn't hidden by other apartment buildings. When I turned my head just a little, I could see my husband resting in a peace that he thought belonged to him.

I sighed. There was no way that I'd ever be able to sleep again. Not as long as Roman was out there and not as long as Kenny didn't know. I just had to tell him. But every time I practiced and played the tape in my mind, I couldn't get past the first part. I couldn't get past saying, "Baby, Sweetheart, Honey, Love of my Life...I have something to tell you: I cheated on you the night before our wedding, and then even after we exchanged vows, that wasn't enough to keep me away from another man."

That was when the tape stopped playing in my head. Not even my subconscious mind wanted to imagine what Kenny's face would look like when he heard that confession. Forget about all the names he would call me – it was the look on his face that I wouldn't be able to handle. The look that would come from a broken heart.

No. I couldn't tell him. I couldn't destroy his life.

Forever. For always.

Kenny and I were going to have our forever. Our for always.

I was going to make sure of it.

But how?

As I sat watching the stillness of the midnight hours outside, I thought about how I'd handled this. For the first time in my life, I was running, and that wasn't like me. I was used to fighting, and I wanted to fight; but how was I supposed to win a battle with a looney-tune? Roman was certifiable, and that meant he would do anything, and go to any extreme, because he didn't care what happened.

That was the advantage he had. He didn't care; he had nothing to lose. I cared and had everything to lose. How was I supposed to fight under those circumstances?

I didn't know, but I had to figure it out. I had to find a way to stop running, turn around, face Roman

and stare that devil straight in his eyes. He needed to
be the one running from me.

But how?

I thought I'd scared him with the police, but
apparently not. I guess he knew I wasn't willing to
take that risk. I needed to get something on him,
something that was equal to what he had on me.

Here was the thing, though – I'd let him into my
world, but I didn't know a thing about his. Besides the
fact that he worked on Muscle Beach and moonlighted
as a stripper, I didn't know anything else. How could I
blackmail with nothing?

Without blackmail, what was left? I needed some
kind of threat. I paused and thought about that.

A threat.

A threat!

I couldn't get out of that chair fast enough. Rushing
into my closet, I scrambled through all of my purses on
the shelf in the back until I found the one that I was
looking for.

"Please, let it be here," I whispered as I checked
every single pocket.

And there it was, in the side panel: the ring and
the card.

How could I have forgotten about this? My eyes
went from the ring to the card, and right there in my
closet, I looked up toward heaven. 'Cause even though
I wasn't living my life anywhere near God, it was clear
that for some reason, He was hanging out about me.

In my hands, I held the keys to my freedom. Kenny
and I were going to have our forever, for always.

Tiptoeing out of the closet, I glanced at the clock. I
wanted to get dressed and dash out of the apartment

right then, but I only had about two hours 'til dawn. I could wait. It would be hard, but I could do it.

I slipped back into bed, tucked the card and the ring underneath my pillow, and laid my head down. And for the first time in a long time, I slept in peace.

Chapter 18

I was up and out before Kenny had even awakened. He was going to be frantic when he woke up and realized I wasn't there; I was sure of that. But hopefully he'd see the note that I'd taped to the bathroom mirror letting him know that I was fine and feeling better and had forgotten about an early meeting. I explained it all: how I was going to catch a cab to work and call another cab at noon so that I could go pick up my car.

My hope was that the note would be enough to keep him calm and to keep him from calling me at work, because he wasn't going to find me there – at least not for the next few hours.

I couldn't make the call from home, so wearing my navy pinstripe corporate suit and the lowest heel pumps I could find in my closet, I trudged down to LaCienega, with the ring and the card in my purse, praying the whole way that the pay phone at the Shell gas station would be working. I was grateful for the early morning breeze, knowing that by nine, the temperature would be above eighty. By the time I walked those five blocks, I had tiny perspiration beads at my temples, but the phone was working and that was all I cared about.

As I dialed the number, I prayed Roman would answer. And on the third ring, he did, sounding groggy but still there.

"Roman, this is Jasmine."

"I knew it was you," he said. "Baby, how are you? I was so worried." He sounded like he was about to crack up with laughter.

I wasn't going to waste a moment with him. "I will pay you to go away, to leave me alone."

"What?"

"Thousands of dollars. I have something that's worth thousands and I'll give it to you."

A pause. "How many thousands?"

My heart started pounding. I hadn't really thought about how much Hines's ring cost, but I took a good guess. "Probably fifteen, maybe twenty thousand dollars."

I heard his whistle through the phone. "Wow, that's a lot of money."

"I know. And it's all yours. I just need you to leave me and my husband alone."

"Like I said, that's a lot of money, but you're worth more than a few thousand to me," he said.

"It's not a few thousand," I yelled, not caring that the two drivers at the gas pumps turned and stared. "Look, Roman," I said. "You really need to take this deal, because one way or the other, this is going to stop."

"Well, I'm glad to hear you want this to end. All we have to do is go back to being together and I'll stop everything." He paused. "Well, not everything, but you know what I'm saying." He laughed. "I'm even willing to make a deal. Since you're married, we don't have to get together every night. Just four or five times a week and I'll be good."

I paused, gritted my teeth, and said, "I'm giving you one more chance, Roman."

He laughed. "You keep threatening me. As if you really could do anything. Anyway, will I see you tonight? Or am I going to see Kenny?"

I slammed down the phone, pissed off that I had even given this fool a chance. But at least I had. And now it was time for me to forget about the ring and focus on the card.

Dumping another quarter into the pay phone, I made the second call, the one I didn't want to make, but the one I had to. In less than five minutes, the arrangements were made.

We'd be meeting at Foxtails at 8:15. Glancing at my watch I had a little more than an hour to wait. There was no way I was going to hang out at this gas station, so I started walking again. There was a Denny's about three blocks away. I would go there. Sit, drink coffee, wait, and plan.

I had given Roman so many chances, and now I was going to come at him with all kinds of guns blazing.

Roman was going to be so sorry that he even thought about messing with me.

⁓⚬⁓

It was eight on the dot when the taxi rolled to a stop.

"You sure this is where you want me to drop you off?" the cab driver asked as he peered through the windshield.

Glancing out, I saw what he saw: the huge, pink letters. Foxtails.

"Yes," I said.

He shook his head, but only a little bit, as if he didn't really want to judge me. I guess he was still trying to figure it out after I paid the meter and slipped out of the cab. To him, I'm sure I didn't look like much of a stripper in my suit. But not looking like a stripper was a good thing.

The door was locked and I had to knock and knock and knock. It took him long enough, but after a few minutes, Buck dragged his big hips to the door.

"You know I don't get up early for nobody," he growled. But then he looked me up and down and grinned. "You've got to be kidding me. You're really trying to go legit?"

"I'm not trying anything," I said, stepping inside of the darkened club. This was the first time that I'd ever been in this place and the music wasn't blasting. It was so quiet it was eerie.

"Ah, come on. When are you gonna stop playing around, Pepper?" Buck asked, refusing to call me by my government name. "Come back to making some real money. Guys are still asking for you."

"What part of "no" don't you understand?"

"What about taking a few dates on the side?" he asked, as if he couldn't hear me. "I could get you some big money. That's how much these cats miss you."

All I did was sigh. The funny thing was, I wasn't tempted at all. What I'd discovered in the last few weeks with Kenny was that love was bigger than all of that.

It had taken me a long time to discover this, but now that I knew, I was going to fight with everything in me for Kenny's love.

"I'm not gonna go back and forth with you, Buck."

He shrugged as he ambled toward the bar. "You're the one who keeps coming back here. I didn't call you."

"I didn't call you either," I said.

He chuckled as he opened a bottle of beer. I shook my head. Buck's morning OJ. He took a swig, then jerked his head toward the red curtain. "He's back there."

"Thanks." With the way I was dressed and with my briefcase in my hand, I felt like I was going to just another early morning business meeting. I pushed back the curtain and stepped inside the VIP lounge. Just like Buck said, Hines was there waiting for me, with two of his boys standing by the back door like they were on lookout.

There was no way for me to stop my grin when I looked Hines up and down. On so many levels, I was so glad to see this man.

"How you doing, baby?" he said as he stepped forward and held me in his arms like he used to.

"I'm good. Well, at least one part of my life is good."

He unbuttoned his expensive jacket, then motioned for me to sit down before he joined me on the velvet couch. When I sat, the hem of my skirt eased up high on my thigh, giving Hines a peek of my thigh-high stockings and garter belt.

He shook his head. "Hmph, hmph, humph! You still got it, baby!"

I waited for that familiar feeling to come over me – the feeling I always got when I was around Hines. The feeling that would've had *me* paying *him* to have sex.

But nothing came. All that was on my mind was Kenny. So the only thing I did was smile.

Hines frowned a little, like he was expecting a different comeback. But that was all I had for him.

"So," he began, "you said you had a little problem?"

I sighed and nodded at the same time.

"What? Ol' boy ain't treating you right?" Hines made a fist with one hand and pounded it into the palm of his other.

"No. No! Kenny is fantastic. He's wonderful. My marriage is great. At least from his end it is. I'm the one who messed up."

His forehead crinkled. "Talk to me, baby. What's up?"

And so I began the story of my infidelity. I told Hines all about meeting Roman at the strip club and then hooking up with him the next day. I told Hines about my wedding and how Roman had shown up and how we'd had hot sex in the bathroom the very next day.

Hines sat, listening intently with not a bit of judgment on his face. His expression didn't change until I got to the part of Roman coming up on me in the parking lot.

My voice was shaky as I relived those moments. "He held me against the car," I said, trying to keep my emotions out of this part of the story too. But it was hard as I remembered just how violated I felt then...and now.

Hines reached for my hand as I told him how I just got in the car afterward and drove away. I explained how distraught I was that I couldn't go to my husband, I couldn't go to the police, I couldn't go anywhere.

"You should've called me, baby."

"I wish I had, because Roman called me that night."

"What?"

I continued, telling him how Roman expected me to still have sex with him and how that's where his threats started.

"He's determined to ruin my marriage." I quivered. When I added the last part about how Roman showed up to the restaurant yesterday and how I'd pretended to faint, Hines held up his hand.

"That's enough," he said.

I was kinda glad he said that; I didn't want to get to the part where I had to tell Hines that I'd offered Roman his ring. I mean, I know for sure that he would've understood, but the thing was, if there was another man that I could've loved besides Kenny, it would've been Hines. From the beginning, Hines touched my heart. He never had sex with me – he made love to me.

When I stopped talking, Hines and I sat there together as he stared at our entwined hands . It was as if he was playing my words over in his head. Like he wanted to understand everything.

Finally, he began nodding his head. "You've been through a lot."

"Yeah, but I brought it on myself," I said, putting my head in my hands. I still had trouble believing that any of this had really happened. "I never planned to sleep with him, and then when I did, I'm telling you, Hines, I never planned to do it again."

"But you just couldn't help yourself, right?"

Ouch! I could only look at him for a moment before I turned my eyes away. Here I was, in the place where I'd slept with hundreds of men, but I was so embarrassed by what was going on now. I guess because it was all just so...stupid.

With the tips of his fingers on my chin, he made me turn back and face him. "What're you ashamed of?"

I shrugged and blinked back tears. "I don't know. It's just crazy. I was barely married twenty-four hours before I had sex with another man."

"I could've told you that was gonna happen, Jasmine," he said as if what I'd done was no big deal. "You're just like me. We love sex too much; we love the variety. That's why I was so shocked when Buck told me that you were going through with your wedding. I never thought it was gonna happen."

"But I love Kenny. I really do."

He chuckled. "I didn't say a word about love. People always get it twisted, always thinking love and sex are the same thing."

What Hines was saying was a fact! I would never be able to explain it, but I just enjoyed the sex. I loved the adoration I felt when men looked at my body. I loved the feelings that tingled through me when they touched me as if I was a precious jewel. And I loved the power. Seeing men raw, naked, broken down to their lowest denomination. When a man released himself, he was totally powerless. At that moment, he would give up anything – and that was when many gave me everything. I'd even had a couple of marriage proposals when my dates' eyes rolled back in their heads as they quivered in ecstasy.

"I wish Kenny understood that," I said. "But he's one of the people who doesn't know the difference between sex and love, and when he hears about Roman...."

"He won't hear about him."

I took a quick breath. This is exactly why I'd come to Hines. "So you'll speak to him for me?" I asked. "Just get him to leave me alone?"

"Yeah, I'll take care of this. He won't bother you again. You got a telephone number for this cat?"

I wondered if Hines really thought he could threaten him on the phone, but I wasn't going to ask any questions. "Yeah," I said, jotting the number down on the back of one of my business cards. "But I don't know anything else about him. I don't know where he lives...all I know is that he works at Muscle Beach and at that strip club."

Hines took the card and nodded as if what I'd given him was enough.

"So," I said slowly, "you'll talk to him, right? All I want is for him to go away."

He looked straight into my eyes. "I'm gonna handle this for you."

I sighed, filled with relief. "I can't thank you...."

He covered my lips with his fingers, stopping me from saying another word. "We're not gonna talk about this anymore. You won't have to worry about Roman contacting you again." I nodded and he said, "But I do want to say, Jasmine, that you can't be getting yourself into these kinds of situations."

I shook my head. "You won't have to worry about me calling you again."

"No, that's not what I'm saying, sweetheart. We're gonna be friends forever. You can call me at any time for anything. What I'm talking about is, even though you won't admit it, I don't put a lot of hope in you staying faithful to your husband."

My eyes got wide.

"Now, listen to me before you start getting all twisted. This is not a judgment; it's a fact. Like I said, you and I are the same. You love sex, baby; you're a freak. And that man you're married to is never going to be able to satisfy you completely. So accept that and be smart."

"I'm never going to cheat on Kenny again." I shook my head so hard, I knew I was gonna have a headache later today.

"Trust me, baby. You're saying that now, and I'm not gonna debate that with you. All I'm trying to do is protect you. You hear me? I'm trying to give you some advice so the next time you find yourself with your thong around your ankles, you won't get caught up in mess like this again."

I was insulted, but I nodded anyway. It wasn't like I could argue Hines down. I mean, look at what I'd done.

He said, "If you're gonna hook up with someone, make sure he has as much to lose as you do."

Okay, at least what Hines was trying to tell me made sense, 'cause that's exactly what I'd been thinking. Roman didn't have anything to lose; I did.

Hines continued: "Handle your business, do what you have to do...but only go after married men. They don't want a relationship, no matter what they say. They got their relationships at home. All they're gonna want with you is sex – the same exact thing that you want."

Even though I knew Hines's words were true, I still felt bad, kinda slimy hearing them. I mean, this felt like a lesson in how to be a successful skank.

"Trust me," Hines said. "I know what I'm talking about."

"Okay."

He kissed the tips of my fingers before he stood, pulling me up with him. Then he hugged me tightly. When he leaned back, he looked into my eyes and said, "You don't have anything else to worry about. Go on home to your husband and hang in there with him for as long as you can. But when that freak starts rising up in you, just remember what I said. Married men, Jasmine. Married men."

This time when he gave me a gentle kiss on my lips, I felt that familiar stirring. What in the hell was wrong with me? I was here, trying to preserve my marriage. And now I was starting to think about sex with Hines.

As if he knew he was holding a fool in his arms, Hines stepped away and strutted toward the back door. Right before he stepped outside, he turned back and blew me a kiss. "Ciao, bella."

I stood there for a moment after he left thanking Hines and God (if He was still listening to me) for getting me out of this mess.

It was over. And I could go and make a life for me and my husband.

Finally.

Chapter 19

It wasn't as though seeing Hines made all of my fear go away. Like I said before, Roman was a special kind of crazy, and I wasn't sure if he would listen to Hines or not. I mean, he *should* listen to Hines. Shoot, the only thing that kept me from being scared of Hines was that I'd seen him whimper like a toddler whenever he had an orgasm. I knew there was a part of his heart that was soft, and it made me doubt some of those hardcore rumors I'd heard about him.

But some of those rumors had to be true, and I was hoping that Hines and his boys would put a whole lotta fear into that empty cavity in Roman's chest where his heart was supposed to be.

My hopes were high when I had Buck call me a cab so that I could get to work. But even when I got to Carnation, rode up in the elevator, and walked into my office, I was careful every step of the way. I probably looked like I'd lost my mind the way I was peeking around corners and looking under desks. Really, I expected Roman to come jumping out of somewhere. I wasn't about to let my guard down.

There was no sign of him, though I knew that didn't mean anything. I'd only left Hines thirty minutes ago; he hadn't had time to catch up with Mr. Crazy yet.

Even though I didn't really think it was funny, I had to chuckle as I thought about that: Mr. Crazy. Roman had gone from Mr. Chocolate to Mr. Crazy in, what, three weeks flat? If I knew then what I know now....

But I couldn't take back what I'd done and Roman couldn't take back what he'd done. So now both of us had to live with the consequences.

For the rest of the morning, I tried to concentrate on work. I had been so off-kilter since I'd gotten married that I was far behind; it was a miracle my boss hadn't been on my case.

I kept one eye on the door and one eye on the phone. But I was not disturbed, and by lunchtime I'd made a little dent in the reports that I had to do. I was on such a roll that I wanted to keep working, but I had to pick up my car. Once I'd done that, I checked in with Kenny to let him know I was okay (and to make sure he hadn't heard from Roman).

"You left so early this morning," Kenny said to me. "But I'm glad you're all right."

"I'm better than all right, baby. I'm just tired of feeling bad, and I'm ready to get to the good part with you."

"I like that." He laughed. "So, do you want a do-over? Try to go out tonight?"

"Naw, with it being Friday, everyone will be out. Let's just stay home," I said, feeling confident that by that time Hines would have met up with Roman and I wouldn't have to worry about Roman ringing my doorbell. "Let's just watch TV and cuddle on the couch."

"That's what I'm talking about."

I knew what I suggested was exactly the kind of night my husband loved. I just had to get used to that boring kind of normal and I would as long as I kept the memory of what had happened with Roman alive. Thinking about what I was going through now would be enough to keep me on the right side of righteousness.

"I'll pick up something for us to eat." I smiled when I added, "At Yee's," which of course was the same-old same-old. But it made Kenny happy.

"I love you, baby."

I laughed; it was so easy to please my husband. Hines may have been a good guy, but he didn't know what he was talking about when it came to me and Kenny. I was gonna love that man for the rest of my life, and for the rest of my life, I was gonna stay true to him.

I was on my way to getting back to happy.

Chapter 20

This was a rare night.

First of all, I was the one who was home – Kenny was not. My husband was taking this real estate licensing seriously and yesterday, he'd found out about a special two-day class down at the Bonaventure Hotel.

When Kenny first told me about it and mentioned that he was going to be staying overnight downtown at the hotel, I wanted to beg him to come home. I'd even thought about jumping into the car with him this morning, though I would've had to answer lots of questions if I'd done that. The thing was, I didn't want to be home by myself.

It had only been three days since I'd spoken to Hines, and though I hadn't heard from Roman, I knew he was there. I could feel his eyes watching me everywhere I went, and I knew he was just waiting for that moment to make his move.

I knew this was paranoia, but it was real to me. I was so paranoid that I'd called Kyla and invited her to come over for a girls' night. And because she was my best friend, Kyla obliged. So here we were, sitting back with our legs stretched out on the coffee table, half-watching the *Cosby* show.

"You really are an old married woman now," Kyla giggled before she sipped her favorite orange and cranberry juice drink. "Just sitting here, doing nothing, hanging out with me."

"What are you talking about? We've been hanging out since kindergarten."

She shook her head. "Nuh-uh. Since we graduated from college, we've hardly spent time together like this."

I kinda shrugged and nodded at the same time. Kyla was right, but it wasn't like I had a lot of girlfriend time over the past few years. I'd been busy — working at Foxtails and doing all of that "entertaining."

"But this is nice and I'm glad you called," Kyla said. Reaching over and touching my hand, she added, "I've missed you."

"Me too," I said, really meaning it.

Kyla and I were as different as ketchup and mustard, but the thing was, this girl was my true friend. From the time we were kids, she never seemed to notice how different we were. It never bothered her that I was a scholarship student. She never cared that my father wore a blue denim shirt and pants to work while her father wore a suit. All Kyla ever saw was me, and that's why she would be my girl until the end of time.

"So, how do you like married life?" she asked, but then she didn't give me a chance to answer. "You don't even have to say anything. I can tell that you love it."

An image of Kenny popped into my mind and all I could do was smile. "Yeah, I do. I'm really happy, Kyla. I never thought I would be this happy."

Kyla waved her hand. "Oh, I knew that you would be. Kenny's your soul mate, just like Jefferson's mine."

"I think you're right."

Kyla twisted around onto the sofa to face me and tilted her head. "What do you mean you think? Didn't you know? Isn't that why you married Kenny?"

I put down my glass filled with lemonade. "I married Kenny because that's what I always wanted to do. And we both know I always get what I want."

"Ha! Don't I know it." Kyla laughed.

"But now I that I'm married, it's more than just wanting Kenny. It's knowing that I'm supposed to be with him."

Kyla nodded as if she understood exactly what I meant. "You know we're two blessed chicks, right?"

Now it was my turn to laugh.

"No seriously," Kyla continued. "Do you know how many women are out there searching for the man God chose for them?"

I tried my best not to roll my eyes, but it was really hard. Kyla was always bringing God into our conversation, and she never seemed to notice that that's when my attention to her exited stage left.

"First of all, they're out of order, because it's the man who finds a wife."

Even though I kept a smile on my face, inside I sighed. I hoped this God-lecture was going to be a short one.

"But besides that," Kyla kept on, "the problem is that women hook up with all of these men, sleeping with this one and that one, and they have no idea that sleeping around will actually stop them from being with the man who's really out there waiting for them."

Okay, so most of the time, I tuned Kyla out when she started acting like a junior-miss-preacher. But obviously, this sleeping around subject was something that I could relate to.

She shook her head. "I wish I could shout it from the rooftops. People just don't know that these soul ties are real."

"Soul ties?" I frowned.

She nodded. "Your soul is supposed to be tied to the man that God has chosen for you. But when you have sex with someone you're not supposed to be with, ungodly soul ties are formed and those things can straight mess you up for real."

I can't really say that I believed in all of this religious goobly-goop. But maybe my heart believed, because it started beating just a little harder.

Kyla lowered her voice as if she didn't want anyone else to hear, even though we were alone. "Pastor Ford has been teaching us all about this, and she said that ungodly soul ties that come from having sex with all of these people can actually fragment your soul so much that eventually, it will make it difficult for you to bond or be joined with anybody. There are women out there who are literally destroying their chances of ever having that relationship they're really looking for."

The men I'd been with flipped through my mind like a deck of flash cards.

"I know you weren't a virgin when you got married," Kyla said, without a hint of judgment in her voice. "I'm just glad that once you met Kenny, that was it for you. Or who knows what would've happened if you'd been out there like that."

She said it like she was relieved, but for me, her words left me a little unsettled. Was the life I'd led the reason why I'd had sex with Roman while on my honeymoon? Had my soul been fragmented like Kyla said? Would I be able to love Kenny the way I wanted to? For the rest of our lives?

I shuddered.

"What's wrong?" Kyla asked.

Before I could answer, the telephone rang, giving me a wonderful reprieve. "I'm going to answer this," I said to Kyla. "It might be Kenny."

"Of course." She waved her hand. "Go on."

Within two seconds, though, I realized it wasn't my husband on the phone.

"Is this a good time?" Hines asked.

I didn't want to talk in front of Kyla, but I couldn't tell Hines to call me back. I had to know now if he'd talked to Roman. I pressed the phone as close to my ear as I could so that no sound would seep out for Kyla to hear. "Yeah, it's good."

Hines said, "I'm gonna keep this short and sweet. You hooked up with a bad dude."

As if he was telling me something I didn't know. Had Hines forgotten what this man had done to me?

But before I could tell him that, he continued, "A woman named Sheri Snow accused him of rape about three months ago, but he was never arrested – at least, not for that one. Another woman, a Marcie Majors, has accused him of the same thing, and there is a warrant out for him for questioning."

In the seconds that it took Hines to give me that news, I played back the scenarios. I remembered the woman at the restaurant at the beach. She couldn't get away from Roman fast enough. Wasn't her name Sheri?

Then there was the way Roman had cut and run from the hotel security guard who found us in the staircase. That man hadn't been five-oh, but Roman probably didn't want to take any chances.

"And you know," Hines said through my thoughts, "there have to be a lot more women out there; these aren't the only two. With you, that makes three. I don't know what else we're gonna find out about this guy, but I can tell you now, it's not going to be good."

"Oh my God!" I could hardly breathe.

Kyla scooted closer to me on the sofa. "Are you okay?" she whispered.

I nodded, though I knew that I looked far from okay.

Through the phone, Hines said, "Sounds like you have company."

"I do."

"Well, I don't talk in front of company."

"But I want to know...."

"There's nothing else you need to know, baby. I got this. Just don't tell anyone that we've talked."

"Okay," I said, but before I had the word totally out of my mouth, I heard the dial tone.

I held the phone to my ear for just a little while longer giving myself time to get steady, to let what I just heard settle in my mind. Finally, I set the phone back in the cradle.

"Jasmine," Kyla whispered my name. "Are you all right?"

I nodded. "Yeah. It's just that I got some news." I shook my head. "But I'm gonna be okay." I took a deep breath. "Yeah, I'm sure of it now. I'm gonna be okay."

And then, my best friend did the thing that made her my best friend – she leaned over and hugged me.

She didn't ask another question or say another word.
Just hugged me.

As we embraced, Hines' words played in my head,
and I realized something: I had been raped. Though I'd
been telling myself that over and over, I'm not sure I
believed it until this moment. But that man had raped
me – and other women too.

All I wanted to do was cry, but I held it in because
Kyla was here. Plus, I didn't have to worry anymore.
Like Hines said, he had me. I was sure that once
Hines talked to him, Roman would never come near
me again.

Especially with what I now knew.

Thank God this was over.

Chapter 21

I was just about ready for my husband to come home.

He'd only been gone for one night, but I missed him so much. Some of it had to do with the news I'd received from Hines, but most of it had to do with the fact that I just liked having my husband around. So I was preparing a welcome-home feast for him: all of his favorites from Yee's, and his favorite drink.

I had the plates set out on the TV trays, our Chinese food in microwave dishes, and now all I had to do was make a pitcher of red Kool-Aid. I had stopped at the store just to get a couple of packages and it was a good thing that I'd bought two because as I tried to tear open the first stupid little package, it ripped and all the red granules tumbled all over the counter. This was why I hated making that stuff; the Kool-Aid always spilled on me.

I was in too good a mood to get upset about anything tonight, though. Kenny was coming home, and with the call from Hines last night, I was free. So I just used my hand to swipe the wasted Kool-Aid off the counter, fixed the other package, and then poured my husband's favorite drink into our wine glasses. I made sure that the Al Green cassette was in the stereo. Of course, I knew that my husband would prefer just sitting down and watching TV right away, but before he did that, he was gonna dance one time with me.

The moment I heard Kenny's key turning in the lock, I cranked up the music, picked up the wineglasses, and did a little two-step to the door.

When my husband walked in, I sang with Al as my backup, "I'm...I'm so in love with you. Whatever you want to do..."

Kenny laughed, dropped his garment bag at the door and took one of the glasses from my hand.

He joined in the song, "It's all right with me...."

It was now a duet as we danced our little hustle together and when Al got to the part of, "I'll never be un...true," I raised my voice so loud you couldn't hear Kenny or Reverend Green.

We rested our glasses on the TV trays and then sang and danced like we were on stage or something, laughing because we both knew that we should only be singing in the shower, but dancing because we were just having fun as man and wife.

This was our forever. Our for always.

When the song ended, we fell onto the couch, giggling so hard, I wondered if we would ever stop. Finally, I caught my breath and picked up my glass. I clicked it against Kenny's and said, "Welcome home, baby."

We both took a small sip of our Kool-Aid, and then Kenny leaned over and gave me a kiss that felt like it would stop my heart. When he finally pulled back, I could hardly breathe.

But he was fine. He said, "I'm gonna go change my clothes and be right back."

"Okay," I said, still gasping. "I'll heat up your plate."

I watched him strut into the bedroom and then I stood and headed into the kitchen. By the time I came back to the living room, Kenny was already slouched back on the couch, with the television on and the remote in his hand.

I smiled. My husband was home.

"Would you look at this?" he said, pointing to the TV and taking his plate from my hand.

I sat as Kenny turned up the volume. The television screen filled with the face of the reporter. "Again, I'm here on Venice Beach," she said, "Muscle Beach actually, the place that Arnold Schwarzenegger made famous."

That was all I needed to hear before my head started spinning.

"Today, one of Muscle Beach's regulars, an unnamed body builder, was found dead, his larynx crushed in an apparent accident when a barbell fell on him as he was doing chest presses."

"See," Kenny said as he waved his fork in the air. "This is why I don't exercise anymore. It's too dangerous."

I couldn't tell if my husband was serious or just trying to make a joke out of this sickly situation. I couldn't tell because I couldn't breathe. I couldn't think. I couldn't speak.

The reporter moved now to the edge of the workout pen where I'd stood talking to Roman just a few weeks ago. "Strangely, the accident occurred in the middle of the day in a crowded area, and yet there are no witnesses to the incident itself. Police are currently investigating...."

I could see the blue uniforms behind her and the yellow tape that sectioned off one part of the workout area.

"...for now, it is being ruled an accident. Police are withholding the name of the victim until relatives can be notified. Back to you in the studio."

"Wow," Kenny said as he picked up a rib and gnawed on the bone. He reached for the remote to turn the channel. "There's gotta be something else on..."

I couldn't even hear the rest of my husband's words. I pushed back my tray and stood up.

"Where you going?"

I pointed toward the bathroom and heard Kenny grunt his acknowledgment. I made it just in time to fall on my knees and wrap my arms around the toilet, just in time to spill my guts, my guilt, my grief.

They had not identified the man, but I knew who it was.

Roman.

Roman was dead.

Because of me.

When there was nothing left inside of me, I sat there and contemplated what had happened, what I had done. I just let the minutes tick by.

Roman was dead.

The floor was cold and hard. Finally, I pushed myself up. It took every bit of energy I had to grab the toilet bowl, then another herculean effort to reach the sink and use that for the final push to stand. When I rose, the first thing that I saw was my face in the mirror.

I stared at myself for a moment; I looked the same, but so much had changed. "Was it because of me?" I asked myself.

As I stood there, my reflection told me no. Roman brought all of this on himself. I'd told him no over and over. Plus, he had raped me.

What was I supposed to do?

I hadn't asked Hines to kill him. Something must've happened. Roman must've said something, done something that pissed Hines off. And from what I heard, you didn't want Hines Gifford upset with you in any kind of way.

Clasping my hands together, I closed my eyes. I wanted to say a prayer or something, to pray for that man's soul, but no words came to me. Maybe it was because I needed to say a prayer for myself first. So all I said was, "I'm sorry," and then stood there, giving Roman his moment of silence.

"Babe, are you okay?" Kenny yelled out. "You didn't fall in or anything, did you?"

I opened my eyes and once again stared at my reflection. "I'm fine," I said keeping my eyes on the mirror. I turned on the faucet, rubbed my hands under the water, but when I looked down I gasped.

There was blood on my hands, dripping into the sink!

I jumped away as if I could get away from my own limbs. But my hands were still with me, red with blood.

Then as I stared at my palms, good sense came back to me. This wasn't blood. This was the Kool-Aid that had spilled earlier.

I fell against the sink, grabbed the soap, and scrubbed my hands until my skin felt raw. I rinsed the sink until it was Kool-Aid free, then turned off the light. Standing in the darkness, I wondered what would come next. What was I supposed to do after I'd had a man murdered? Was I supposed to call Hines? Thank him? But in that instant, I knew I would never see Hines again.

"Babe?"

"I'm coming," I said as I stepped out from the bathroom.

My husband wanted me in the living room with him so that we could spend our Friday night watching mindless sitcoms and sharing fortune cookies. And I was going to do that. From now on, this was going to be my life. No matter what, I would live it and I would love it.

This was my forever. My for always. Never again would trouble find me.

I strolled back into the living room as if a man being dead wasn't my fault. But just before I took my rightful place next to my husband, words echoed in my mind.

"We love sex too much; we love the variety."

Why were the words that Hines had said to me all up in my head? No one ever had to worry about me cheating on my husband again. Not after all I'd been through.

"You love sex, baby; you're a freak. And that man you're married to is never going to be able to satisfy you completely."

I shook those thoughts away and smiled at Kenny.

"You okay?" my husband asked.

I nodded. "Yeah, I'm good. I'm exactly where I want to be."

"Oh, yeah?" He grinned.

"Yeah," I said, taking his hand. "Forever, for always."

"Handle your business, do what you have to do...but only go after married men."

Hines words continued to taunt me, and I continued to ignore them, replacing his words with my own promises never to cheat again.

But though I tried and I tried and I tried, Hines's words turned out to be much more prophetic than mine.

The End

Here's a sneak peek of FRIENDS & FOES by Victoria Christopher Murray and ReShonda Tate Billingsley, coming February 2013!

FRIENDS & FOES

God has a great sense of humor.

Rachel Jackson Adams could remember her mother's words as if she'd uttered them yesterday. When Rachel was growing up, it was one of the sayings Loretta Jackson loved most.

Well, God must be some kind of comedian because this had to be the biggest joke of all.

"Why are you sitting there with your mouth wide open?"

Rachel jumped at the sound of Lester's voice. She'd been so engrossed in the email she'd just read, she hadn't even heard her husband come in the house.

Rachel didn't bother to speak as she shook her head in disbelief. "This is unbelievable," she muttered, more to herself than to him as she leaned back in the leather office chair.

Lester set down his briefcase, walked over, and kissed his wife on the head. "What's unbelievable? Macy's is having a going-out-of-business sale? Dillard's is closing early?" he joked.

The evil eye she flashed at him wiped the smile right off his face. After nine years of marriage,

Lester knew when his wife was about to lose it and she was definitely on the verge right now.

"Okay, babe, what's going on? You look like you're about to explode," Lester asked, all traces of laughter gone.

"I am," Rachel snapped. She spun her laptop around to face him. "Look at this mess."

Lester peered at the screen. "Okay, it's an email."

"No kidding." She jabbed a manicured nail at the screen. "It's an email from Yvette."

"Who is Yvette?"

She huffed and rolled her eyes. "Good grief, Lester, the publicist for the American Baptist Coalition. You know, the woman we hired."

"Okay, calm down," Lester said as he continued reading. "I just didn't immediately realize who you were talking about." When he got to the end of the email, a huge grin spread across Lester's face. "That is phenomenal."

Rachel popped her husband upside the back of his head. "Wow, what did you do that for?"

"What do you mean, it's phenomenal?"

He looked at her, confused. "Oprah isn't phenomenal?" She didn't answer, just kept glaring at him like he'd done something wrong. "Sweetheart, I don't understand," he continued. "The American Baptist Coalition is about to be represented on Oprah and you're upset about that?"

"You doggone right, I'm upset," Rachel said, slamming the laptop shut. "Why in the world is she going on Oprah?"

"Lady Jasmine?" he asked, still bewildered.

"Her name ain't no damn *Lady* Jasmine!" Rachel yelled. "I told you to stop calling her that.

Call her *Shady* Jasmine, Jas, Jazzy, shoot, call her Pepper Pulaski after the name she used to use when she was a stripper for all I care, but stop calling her that like she's some type of royalty!"

Lester took a deep breath, trying to stay calm in order to keep her calm. "Okay, let's back up because I really don't understand your anger."

Her husband really and truly could work her nerves sometimes. He could be so naïve. Granted, over the years he'd gotten a little backbone and since he'd become a popular preacher, his confidence had soared. It had gone to even greaterheights when he'd won the election for the presidency of the American Baptist Coalition six months ago. That had been a brutal fight – not between Lester and the man he was running against, Pastor Hosea Bush, but between Rachel and Pastor Bush's wife, Jasmine. Things had gotten downright ugly between the two of them, but at the end of the day, Rachel had emerged victorious. Just like she knew she would.

And for the first four months, Rachel had been the shining star of the ABC. She'd increased their visibility, convinced them to hire the publicist, streamlined some of their programs, introduced a few others, and had worked around the clock to make the ABC even more powerful than it already was.

So why in the world was Jasmine the one going on Oprah?

"I'm the first lady of the American Baptist Coalition," Rachel slowly said. "If O is gonna be talking to anybody, she needs to be talking to me."

Lester pointed at the email. "But Yvette said Jasmine will be talking about the new community center she's starting, Jacqueline's Hope."

"I don't care what she's talking about. It's. *Oprah.* The only person that should be talking to Oprah on behalf of the ABC is me! I'm in the driver's seat. Jasmine is back in the bed of the pickup truck. So why is it that every time I turn around, Jasmine don't-nobody-wanna-say-all-them-dang-last-names is getting all the attention?"

That brought a small smile to Lester's face. "Bush. Her name is Jasmine Bush." He chuckled. "As if you didn't know."

Rachel waved him off. "She's been married thirty times so I can't keep up. Why are you taking up for her, anyway?" The disdain Rachel held for Jasmine was no secret. The bougie, over-the-top troll had caused her enough headaches to last a lifetime.

"Rachel, you get your fair share of press, too," he said, soothingly. "You just did a TV appearance last week."

"Yeah, on Fox 26 News. That's local. I'm a global type of woman and I'm resigned to local press? That's unacceptable."

"Oh, you're global now." He laughed.

Rachel stood, her hands plastered on her hips. Sure, this type of thing didn't used to be her forte, particularly since she had been a reluctant first lady. But after some rough patches, she'd come to like the power that came along with being an esteemed first lady. "Lester Eugene Adams, I don't see anything funny."

He immediately wiped the smile off his face. "Sweetheart," he said gently, "this really is good news."

Rachel relaxed a bit, even though her anger didn't subside. "Why is she always trying to steal my thunder? We won this election fair and square, yet she has been the bane of my existence for the past few months. She thinks because she has Moses' mama on her side, she can just take over."

Lester sighed. "You promised to stop talking about Mae Frances like that."

Rachel didn't even want to get into a debate with Lester about that crazy old woman who walked around in a matted full-length mink coat that she probably got at an estate sale in 1967. The Bushes claimed that Mae Frances was just a family friend, but something about that old woman turned Rachel's stomach.

"Lester, I don't care about that old hag – or Mae Frances," Rachel quipped.

"I thought you and Jasmine were getting along," Lester replied.

"No, Jasmine recognized that she lost the election fair and square. And I thought not hearing from her for four months meant that she was gracious in defeat. But she was just plotting to see how she could steal my shine."

After the election, Jasmine had all but disappeared – thankfully. She'd hadn't even bothered to reply to the email Rachel sent asking if Jasmine wanted to be her assistant. Then last month, out of the blue, she'd sent the board a press release talking about the center she was opening in honor of her little girl who'd been kidnapped. As a mother, Rachel could sympathize with not knowing where your child was. But they'd found the little girl, and still Jasmine milked sympathy every chance she could.

Rachel felt disrespected because Jasmine hadn't even bothered to talk to her about the center. Then, she'd gone over Rachel's head and contacted the ABC ladies' auxiliary about hosting a fundraiser. Now, she thought she was about to give the ultimate disrespect and go on Oprah? By herself? Oh, hell no. Not if Rachel had anything to say about it!

"You do realize this is not the first time they've done something like this," Rachel replied. "Do I need to remind you of the article about Hosea on Essence.com last week?"

"That was about his TV show getting syndicated."

"And did they or did they not mention his role in the ABC? Yet, they didn't bother to mention your name, Mr. President, at all."

"Honey, this isn't about me. Or you. This is about the ABC. One of the things we promised to do was bring more positive coverage. I think it's wonderful that Jasmine is helping us do that."

He stepped toward her and tried to take her hand. Rachel snatched it away. Sometimes she wished she could jump into her husband's body and take it over. He could be so doggone passive-aggressive. But that was okay, she thought to herself. That's why he had her.

"Fine, Lester. I'm going to start dinner. My dad will be back with the kids any minute now."

Lester grabbed her hand and stopped her. "Are you good?"

"I'm great," she said, feigning a smile. Rachel left the room and instead of going right into their oversized kitchen, she went left, up the spiral staircase and into her bedroom. She grabbed her purse, pulled her credit card out of her wallet, and snatched her cell phone off the nightstand. She punched in the number she knew by heart.

"Continental Airlines, may I help you?" the voice said.

"Yes . . . I need a ticket to Chicago . . ." Rachel smiled as she leaned back against her headboard. She thought Jasmine had learned that she wasn't the one to be played with, but it looked like ol' Jazzy needed to be reminded of that. So, let the games begin!

The End

⚬⁓⚬

Victoria Christopher Murray is the *Essence* bestselling author of THE DEAL, THE DANCE, AND THE DEVIL; LADY JASMINE; SINS OF THE MOTHER; TOO LITTLE, TOO LATE; DESTINY'S DIVAS and other novels. Visit her at www.VictoriaChristopherMurray.com.

Made in the USA
San Bernardino, CA
23 March 2014